CAROLINE CORBY was born and brought up in London. She studied mathematics and statistics at Bristol University, then became a banker and spent thirteen years in the City, ending up as a director in a venture capital company before deciding to leave her job to spend more time with her young family.

Caroline has always enjoyed history and wanted to find a historical novel aimed at children that would capture her daughters' imagination. After searching without success, she decided to write one herself and the Before They Were Famous series was born. It explores the early lives of some of history's most fascinating characters who, in shifting, dangerous worlds, struggle to make their mark and become heroes and heroines of the future. Of *Julius Caesar: The Curse of the Gods*, Caroline says: "I was intrigued to find out more about Caesar's childhood. I'm convinced it is the key to his extraordinary life."

Caroline lives in Hampstead, North London, with her husband and three daughters, aged seventeen, fifteen and twelve.

Other titles in the series

CAROLINE CORBY

JULIUS CÆSAR

THE CURSE OF THE GODS

**WALKER
BOOKS**

First published in Great Britain 2011 by Walker Books Ltd
87 Vauxhall Walk, London SE11 5HJ

2 4 6 8 10 9 7 5 3

Text © 2011 Caroline Corby
Cover design © 2011 Walker Books Ltd

This book has been typeset in Quercus, Usherwood and Herculanum

Printed in Great Britain by Clays Ltd, St Ives plc

British Library Cataloguing in Publication Data:
a catalogue record for this book is
available from the British Library

ISBN 978-1-4063-1254-6

www.walker.co.uk

For my parents,
John and Barbara Mills

DECEMBER, 89 BC
ANCIENT ROME

1

"IT'S snowing, Gaius. Go and have fun. You can finish that translation at home."

Gratefully Gaius Julius Caesar dropped his stylus and jumped up from the bench where he'd been studying since dawn. Like all boys from the Julii clan he was tall with fair skin, dark curly hair and piercing brown eyes.

"Thank you," he said, grinning excitedly. He quickly tied a heavy cloak over his blue tunic and slipped on the leather shoes he'd left by the door.

"You'll need these if you're to make a decent snowball," said his elderly tutor, tossing over a pair of sheepskin mittens. "Now be off with you. Snow is a rare treat in Rome."

Gaius ran down the rickety steps from Gnipo's apartment two at a time. Flakes were falling from the leaden sky and already the ground was dusted white.

He darted through a narrow archway into the busy alleys of the Subura, Rome's poorest district, and then turned sharply left, hurrying past tatty apartments, haphazardly balanced one on top of another, towards the only walled villa in the lane. As he approached its gate a lanky dog with wiry grey fur began to bark.

"Calm down, Canis," he called. "I'm off to the field. I'm not coming home yet."

"Yes, you are!" His mother stepped out from the doorway. Aurelia Cotta was also tall, with a long nose, high forehead, and lips painted a startling shade of scarlet. Her dangling earrings caught on her shoulders and she was fussily dressed in a red linen gown, matching tunic and a gauze veil. "Come inside!"

"But what about the snow?"

"Leave it. I have something important to tell you." She pulled him close and whispered, "A vestal is in disgrace. Those priestesses are forbidden to see men but she was caught alone with one. And the worst thing is, it's Calpurnia Cotta. She's a cousin so it could be a dangerous time for the family until she's punished."

Inwardly Gaius groaned. For years the Julii had been a leading family in Rome but they had fallen on hard times and Aurelia was determined to improve things. Every meal, they set food aside for the gods and frequently they made offerings at the temple. But not today, thought Gaius. *Not now, when it's snowing for the first time in years.*

"I won't be long," he pleaded. "I only want to go to the field and I promise to be careful."

But his mother shook her head.

"No. That's not good enough. You must stay at home. Only once the Temple of Vesta is blessed will it be safe for any Julii to go outside again."

"When will that be?"

"Tomorrow, before dawn."

"But by then the snow may have melted."

"Then you'll miss it. Now come inside and make an offering. You're in danger of provoking the gods."

Resignedly Gaius trudged after his mother across a scruffy courtyard. It had a brown and white mosaic floor, patched in places, and was overshadowed by tenement blocks. On the far side they entered a cramped chamber. Here Aurelia opened the doors of a small wooden box fixed to the wall. Inside the family altar was a statue of their ancestor, the goddess Venus, cut from milky white stone. Although the statue was tiny, Venus was intricately carved with earrings, pleats in her long dress and minute outstretched hands.

"Beg the gods to bless the Julii," Aurelia ordered her son as she handed him a shiny date, "and respectfully remind Venus that we haven't seen Calpurnia Cotta for many years."

Gaius placed the fruit at the goddess's feet. He tried to put the frustration of being cooped up at home from his mind as he began to pray, but suddenly he felt a piercing pain, as if an invisible band was being tugged tight around his forehead.

"Gaius, are you all right?" asked his mother.

But he couldn't answer. The room began to spin, his knees buckled and he collapsed to the floor.

* * *

"Gaius, can you hear me? Talk to me!"

Gaius's head was throbbing, his mouth tasted strangely metallic, every muscle ached and he felt wearier than he'd ever felt before.

"Gaius! Are you awake?"

Someone shook him. Whoever it was, they were not going to let him rest. Groggily he opened his eyes. Despite the bitter cold his forehead felt damp and sticky. It took him a moment to focus but gradually he became aware that he was in a gloomy room lit by a single candle. He looked around – he was lying on his mother's bed and she was perched beside him, pale as marble.

"What happened? Did I faint?" he asked weakly.

"I wish you had."

Aurelia began to pace the room.

Despite his exhaustion, Gaius pulled himself up onto his elbows. "Mother, what is it?"

She glared at him. "You were writhing like a snake! I warned you not to trifle with the gods, and now look what's happened! You've upset them and they've taken their revenge."

"What do you mean?"

"A demon possessed you. You've been cursed!"

2

GAIUS felt as though he'd been kicked in the stomach. He knew the gods sent seizures and madness to those who displeased them. But what had he done wrong?

"Why would the gods curse me?" he asked his mother.

"Perhaps it was your reluctance to pray!" Aurelia shook her head disapprovingly. "Quintus would never have behaved so badly."

Gaius's spirits sank still further. His mother was right; his elder brother always did as he was told. Not only that, Quintus was handsome, an excellent scholar and an impressive athlete – in fact, everything Gaius was not.

"And what a time to choose," continued his mother. "You'll ruin his celebrations."

In two days' time Quintus would become a Roman citizen and Aurelia had spent months planning the festivities.

"I'm sorry," said Gaius wretchedly. "Would it help if I made another sacrifice to the gods? I could give them the bow and arrow Father gave me last time he was home."

"A toy! They would be insulted!" snapped his mother, her scarlet lips tight with anger. "Because of you I'll have to spend a fortune when we've precious little money to spare. In the morning we'll visit the Temple of Vesta. I'll need to offer a goat at the very least, perhaps even a lamb, if we're to have any chance of persuading the gods to be merciful. Until then, don't leave this room!"

"Why?"

Aurelia shook her head so vigorously her earrings jangled. "Don't you understand? I know we're poor now but when Quintus becomes a man, we have a chance to get back to where we belong. But it won't happen if rumours spread that a Julii is cursed. So stay here, out of sight, while I make the arrangements."

Taking the only candle, Aurelia crossed the room to a large chest chained to the floor. She pulled a ring of keys from her belt, unlocked it and began searching for her money pouch.

Perhaps it was being in the gloomy shadows but Gaius was overcome with weariness once more. His head sank to the pillow and he felt almost desperate for sleep, but he had that distracting metallic taste in his mouth.

"Mother, could you ask a slave to bring me water?" he asked as Aurelia stood up, clutching several gold coins.

"I'll send Flora later but no one else must see you. It's too risky. Slaves gossip too much."

His mother left and Gaius lay back down, but he couldn't sleep. It was not only the strange taste in his mouth, it was knowing that a demon had possessed him. Could it return? And if so, when? He rolled on to his side and tried to settle but his mind was whirring. Gradually the light outside faded and still he couldn't rest. Then something creaked in the far corner of the room. His heart began to pound. Was the fiend back already? There it was again. The sound was coming from behind his mother's chest.

He sat up. "Who's there?"

But instead of a fiend, out crawled a girl. She was about his age, and was short with a snub nose, hollow cheeks and patches of black stubble on her otherwise bald head.

"Who are you?" he asked.

"My name is Zoe, master." She spoke quietly and with a foreign accent. "I'm new to your household. I arrived yesterday."

Gaius remembered his mother mentioning last night that she had bought a brother and sister in the market. At seven hundred sestertii, Aurelia had declared, they were a bargain. The girl would help Flora, the cook slave, in the kitchen while the older boy had been sent to her brother-in-law as a gift.

"Why are you hiding in here?" Gaius asked.

"I was in the courtyard, master, when the mistress dragged you out. I hid behind a pillar but you looked so strange I was frightened, so I ran to the nearest room. When your mother carried you in here, I nearly fainted. Honestly, master, I didn't mean to pry."

"But you heard everything," said Gaius slowly. "For that, Mother could have you killed."

The girl fell to her knees. "I'll never say a word. I was caught by a slave-dealer less than a month ago and brought straight to Rome. I don't know anyone in the city to gossip to. Please, master!"

Just then the door opened and there was Flora holding a jug of water and a cup, followed by Aurelia.

"Zoe, what are you doing here?" Aurelia asked sharply.

The girl began to shake and, even though she was just a slave, Gaius felt sorry for her. Perhaps it was because they were about the same age or maybe it was that she looked so fragile with her skinny arms and shorn scalp, but he didn't want her to get into trouble.

"Mother, Zoe just came to ask your permission to buy eggs in the market," he fibbed.

"Eggs! What do I care about eggs?" snapped Aurelia. "Flora, put that water down and take Zoe away. Now!"

"Yes, mistress," said the old cook slave, shooing Zoe from the room.

"Slaves! Sometimes I wonder if they are more trouble than they're worth," sighed Aurelia, as she poured Gaius a cup of water. "Flora complained when I sent her to buy a lamb. And she's been moody ever since I bought Zoe."

"Why?" asked Gaius, happy to distract his mother from his own disgrace.

"Flora's getting old. This spring she'll have worked for us for twenty years and she was hoping that I'd grant her her freedom, but a new cook would cost a fortune. With Zoe's help, Flora can keep going for a few more years."

Flora had been captured in North Africa by Gaius's father and brought back by him to Rome. Over the years she had graduated from being the most junior slave in the household to the most senior. From her lair in the kitchen she bossed the other slaves about and although she was reasonably polite to her mistress, she still treated Gaius and Quintus like naughty toddlers.

"But she dreams of going home," said Gaius. "She's been talking of nothing else for months."

Aurelia pursed her lips. "Well, she is just going to have to wait a while longer. Anyway, forget about the slaves. Their affairs are so tiresome. What you must remember is not to do anything to anger the gods until that lamb is sacrificed. Do you understand?"

"Yes, Mother," said Gaius, trying to put Zoe and the lie he had just told to the back of his mind.

3

JUST after dawn the next morning, Gaius and his mother stepped into the frosty courtyard. Despite the early hour and the freezing temperature, they were dressed in their finest clothes. Aurelia wore a pale yellow robe and cape of Egyptian linen, and overnight Flora had dyed her hair an alarming shade of ginger.

At his mother's insistence Gaius wore red leather shoes and a toga bordered with a crimson stripe – clothes only aristocrats were permitted to wear. However, he didn't look as elegant as his mother had hoped because the toga, which had belonged to Quintus, was fraying and patched, and although Gaius was tall for his age it was still too long, drowning him in yards of trailing cloth.

"I suppose you'll have to do," sighed Aurelia. She pointed to a small lamb with tight black curls tied to a post by the kitchen door. "Pick it up. It cost four sestertii, so mind you hold on tight."

Gaius wedged the bleating animal under his arm as best he could, earning a few sharp kicks in his ribs for his trouble.

"Canis, be quiet!" Aurelia snapped at the yapping guard dog. "And Gaius, be careful with your bulla. The last thing we need is that getting lost."

He glanced down. One of the lamb's hooves had somehow got tangled in the leather thong tied around his neck and had fallen off. He picked up the necklace and then squeezed the drawstring pouch. Inside was a reassuring round metal disc – a solid gold charm. Every Roman boy wore one. The charms warded off evil and were treasured objects, passed from one generation to the next. As the eldest son, Quintus wore his father's, but Gaius's was also special. It had belonged to his uncle, General Marius, a leading soldier in Rome.

"It's safe," he said, retying the knot.

"I should hope so. Marius may ask to see it at the games on Martis. Men can be sentimental about the charms they wore as boys."

They left the peace of the courtyard and went out into the alleys, where street vendors, fortune tellers, musicians and beggars were already setting up stalls for the day ahead.

"I loathe this district," moaned Aurelia when moments later her pristine dress was splashed with flecks of mud. "When I married a Julii, I never imagined I'd end up living in this dump."

Inwardly Gaius bristled. His mother constantly blamed his father for the family's poverty. He had spent years away from home fighting in the Roman army but however much money he sent back it was never enough to satisfy his wife. Aurelia would not be happy until she could afford to move back to the luxury of the Palatine Hill where she had grown up.

"Not everyone owns a mansion on the Hill," Gaius murmured out of loyalty to the father he hadn't seen for two years.

"We're not everyone, Gaius. We are the Julii. Now hurry up or we'll be late."

It wasn't long before they emerged from the filthy alleys of the Subura district into the wide open Forum, the centre of Rome. One side of the huge square was lined with grand temples dedicated to the gods Jupiter, Mars, Castor and Pollux. Each temple had vast marble columns, bronze doors and hundreds of gold statues glinting in the watery sunlight. On the opposite side was the imposing Senate building, where distinguished senators passed new laws, and in between was the rostrum, a round stone stage where any citizen could make a speech.

"This way," said Aurelia, striding purposefully towards the eastern corner of the square. Tucked beyond the Senate was the Temple of Vesta, a small round building where a sacred flame burned day and night, protecting Rome. Behind this was the much larger Palace of the Vestals, home to the city's leading priestesses.

"What are you here for?" asked an old woman as Aurelia and Gaius sat down on the palace steps.

"A blessing," said Aurelia shortly.

"Me too. My daughter has a baby on the way and wants to be sure it's a boy. I've been here since before dawn.

Hopefully a vestal should be along soon."

"I wouldn't count on it," moaned a sallow man in a tunic that had seen better days. "I've promised these two their freedom." He pointed at a couple of elderly slaves. "I thought it would be quicker than going to the notary, but now I'm not so sure."

Aurelia ignored him. She hated it when ordinary people spoke to her as if she were one of them. It annoyed her that she couldn't afford the necklaces and silks that would instantly mark her out as an aristocrat and someone to be treated with respect.

"How can a vestal free slaves?" Gaius asked, embarrassed by his mother's rudeness.

"Just by her touch. These two have served me for years. It's about time I let them go, but I should have gone to the notary instead."

"Don't give up. There's one coming now," said the old woman, pointing at a carriage with a gleaming white hood on the far side of the Forum. She hurried towards the front of a crowd forming by the temple doors, with Aurelia only a step behind.

The carriage drew up and out stepped a woman in a long white flowing robe. A veil covered her face and a pale mantle was pinned at her left shoulder with a silver brooch. Gracefully she climbed the steps, announcing, "We can only see one person today."

Many hands went up, begging for attention. *We don't stand a chance*, thought Gaius, hurrying to catch up with his mother. In his haste he tripped over his toga, and the lamb wriggled free and bolted into the crowd. Without thinking Gaius dived and grabbed its foot. When he looked up he was horrified to find the vestal staring down at him through her gauze veil.

"Why are you here?" she asked.

Gaius's cheeks burned. "I need a blessing from the chief vestal."

"Then follow me."

"Thank you, madam," said Aurelia, pushing herself forward. "We're most grateful."

"I said only one person," replied the vestal. "Who needs the blessing? You or the boy?"

"The boy," admitted Aurelia.

"Then wait here with everybody else."

Quickly Aurelia pulled Gaius close. "Don't say a word about the demon. Remember, priestesses gossip as much as everybody else."

"Is he coming?" asked the vestal. "Or should I choose another?"

"He's coming," said Aurelia, pushing her son up the stairs.

Respectfully, Gaius pulled a length of his toga up to cover his head and followed the woman through grand doors into a large chamber with grey marble walls.

"I'm Vestal Marta," she said, lifting her veil. She was younger than he'd realized, probably only fifteen years old, with blue eyes, straight teeth and milky skin that looked like it had never seen the sun. "You want to see Mistress Fulvia Pollo?"

"Yes, please."

"Who should I say has come?"

"Gaius Julius Caesar."

"Of the Julii clan?" Marta looked at him curiously. "Then we're related. I'm from the Publius branch of the family. And you?"

"General Marius is my uncle and my father commands the Eighth Legion," Gaius answered, just as another woman swept into the room.

She was dressed in the same white robes as Marta but was much older, with a beaky nose, a wrinkled, pallid face and wrists so tiny they looked like they could snap.

"Marta, where have you been?" she said sharply. "I've been looking for you all morning."

"I was summoned by the Consul's household," murmured the young vestal, her eyes respectfully to the ground.

"Again? What was it this time – a servant frightened by the entrails of a chicken? Now who is this?"

"Gaius Julius Caesar."

"What does he want?"

"I don't know, ma'am."

"Leave this to me. You search the building. That girl must be found."

They must be talking about Calpurnia Cotta, the

disgraced vestal, thought Gaius. *Has she gone missing?*

"Ma'am, I know you're angry with her, but perhaps things were not as they seemed," said Marta quietly.

"I refuse to discuss this matter further," snapped Fulvia Pollo. "Do you want everyone to know our business?"

"But..."

"I'm warning you, Marta – not another word. Now, go!"

"Every girl is the same," said Fulvia Pollo as the young vestal left. "It takes them at least twelve months to settle, if they settle at all, and many years to understand the importance of their sacred duties. Now you can see I'm busy. Tell me quickly, Gaius Julius Caesar, why are you here?"

"My mother, Aurelia Cotta, wishes that I ask for a blessing."

"Why?"

"The disgraced vestal is a cousin of ours. Mother worries it may be an unlucky time for the family so she thought it best to make an offering."

He held out the lamb and for the first time Fulvia Pollo glanced at the animal. "So that's it? There's nothing more to this visit?"

She stared at Gaius with her piercing brown eyes and he had the uncomfortable sensation that she knew he wasn't telling her everything. But his mother had warned him not to mention the curse, so he murmured, "No. Mother just likes to be cautious."

"Then come this way."

Holding up his toga, Gaius followed the old woman

down a long corridor and through several gloomy rooms. At last they reached a chamber lit by one flaming torch with black stone walls and a thick red stripe painted across the ceiling.

"Sit there while I go to the temple," said the chief vestal, pointing at a wooden bench. "And give me the lamb."

As he held out the creature, it began to buck wildly, as though sensing its fate.

"Watch out. Your pouch has fallen off."

"That's strange," said Gaius, picking it up from the stone floor. "That's twice in one day and it's never happened before."

Fulvia Pollo looked thoughtful. "Perhaps this is an inauspicious time for the Julii. I'll see what the sacred flame has to say. Now, wait and don't be tempted to wander off. Many rooms here are forbidden to men... even ones as young as you."

The dismal chamber was dark and cold. Gaius pulled his toga close but the damp still made him shiver. He waited for what felt like forever in the windowless gloom until at last he heard footsteps. But instead of Fulvia Pollo, a worried-looking girl came in, glanced quickly round and hurried off, too terrified to catch his eye. Gaius couldn't help feeling sorry for her. What must it be like to be picked at nine or ten years old to be a vestal priestess, knowing you would spend the next thirty years in this place and that if you broke any of its strict rules you'd be buried alive? He was surprised they hadn't all fled like

Calpurnia Cotta. He'd only been here a morning and was already desperate to leave.

"Did you think I'd forgotten you?" Fulvia Pollo appeared from nowhere, making him jump. "It always takes longer when I'm not told the whole story."

She smeared his forehead with something warm and sticky – the blood of the lamb.

"The flame told me of your curse. You're cleansed for now but I'm warning you, it will return."

The gods must have told her what had happened! And to make it worse they were not going to leave him in peace. Before he could stop himself Gaius blurted out, "Will it come again soon?"

"It will come when it pleases."

"What can I do?"

"Live in fear and hide yourself away or prove yourself worthy despite this affliction. You must choose."

"How can I prove myself worthy?"

The old woman shrugged unsympathetically. "I've told you all I can. Give this to your mother."

She handed him a metal plate. He tilted it towards the torchlight and read out loud, "'The Julii will rise when the last egg hatches.'"

"What does it mean?" he asked.

The ancient vestal scowled. "You ask too many questions, Gaius Julius Caesar. Be on your way. I have no more to say to you."

And she left without another word.

4

NOW that he was alone, Gaius felt even more frightened. The curse would return... He had to prove himself worthy. But how? He was only eleven years old. He shuddered. The temple was so gloomy. Perhaps he would feel better in sunlight. He began to retrace his steps, his shoes echoing along the stone corridor.

"*Psst.*"

He swung round, heart thudding.

"*Psst.*"

There it was again. Could it be the demon? He wanted to run away but forced himself to stop.

"Come here," said a voice, and a face poked out from behind a pillar. It was Marta, the girl who'd brought him into the temple.

"What is it?" he asked, feeling foolish that he'd been so frightened.

She grabbed his wrist and pulled him behind the column. "Keep your voice down, or we'll both be in trouble. I can help you ... if you'll help me."

"How?"

"I want you to deliver a message. It's to a man called Rufus Agrippa. He's a Tribune and he lives on the Palatine

Hill but no one must know."

Gaius was baffled. "Why me?"

"*I* can't be seen with men ... even a boy like you. Just tell Rufus, 'Meet at the steps of the Temple of Castor and Pollux at sunset this Saturni.' And make sure no one else hears. Can you do that?"

"Maybe," said Gaius doubtfully, for it wouldn't be easy to cross Rome and back without his mother demanding to know where he had been.

"If you agree, I'll help you interpret the prophesy Fulvia Pollo made for your mother."

The prophesy! Gaius had almost forgotten the riddle on the tin plate, but he knew his mother would think it was important so he added, "Tomorrow my brother becomes a citizen, but I could go the next day."

"Good." The vestal smiled briefly. "When Fulvia Pollo consulted the flames she said that the last egg was the seventh egg but keep that to yourself or I'll be in trouble."

She gave Gaius a sharp push and he found himself back in the middle of the corridor.

"Still here?"

It was Fulvia Pollo, walking towards him, looking suspicious.

"I'm just leaving," he said hastily.

"Good. Don't let me catch you hanging around again."

After the gloom of the temple, the Forum was reassuringly bright and busy. In one corner men were selling slaves straight from the port. Around twenty girls were linked by chains, their heads shaved and their tunics grubby and torn. On the rostrum a town crier was booming out a list of candidates in the upcoming election. Shopkeepers were selling food, money lenders were busy with their scales and snake charmers were playing flutes to make their cobras dance.

Gaius searched the crowds for his mother and soon spotted her sitting on a bench by a fountain, her cape pulled close.

"You were ages," she complained. "My hands are freezing." And then she noticed the blood on his forehead. "What did Fulvia Pollo say?"

Suddenly Gaius realized he couldn't tell her the truth. The vestal had said that it was for him alone to overcome the curse. His mother couldn't help.

"Gaius, tell me – was it bad news?"

"No. Not bad news," he answered. "I am cleansed. The gods will not bother me again for a long time."

"A long time? Not never?"

To say never felt like too much of a lie so he shook his head. "No. But not for a long time."

"I suppose that's the best we can hope for. Anything else?"

He handed her the tin plate and his mother scrutinized it carefully.

"What does it mean? The vestal must have given you a clue."

"No," he replied, wishing he could tell her about the seventh egg.

Aurelia read the words out loud. "The Julii will rise when the last egg hatches." And then she smiled. "We *will* rise. You and Quintus have divine blood and Venus will see to it. I feel it in my bones."

Not unless I find a way to deal with this curse, thought Gaius, but he hadn't the heart to tell her.

5

EARLY the next morning Quintus sat patiently on a couch in the dining room while a slave cut his hair. He was a lanky boy with strong shoulders and the beginnings of a downy moustache, and for the first time he was dressed in a tunic and a toga virilus – the off-white plain toga of a man.

The slave carefully cut one final curl.

"What do you think?" Quintus asked.

Gaius couldn't believe the change. All children had long hair. Now that his brother's was gone, Quintus looked grown up.

"I hardly recognize you," he admitted.

"That's because he's almost a man," said Aurelia proudly. "Just the charm to go and it's done."

With a dagger she sliced through the thong hanging from her eldest son's neck and tipped the golden charm out of its bag. Carefully she wrapped it in a piece of linen, opened the family altar and laid it at the feet of the tiny statue of Venus.

"This charm has protected Quintus since he was nine days old, as it protected his father and his grandfather before him," she said. "Now he is old enough to look after

31

himself I give it back to you for safekeeping. But Venus, on this special day, please hear my prayers. The Julii have suffered for too long. I know my husband has not distinguished himself, but, with your help, my son can. Surely now that Quintus is safely grown we should not have to wait too long before the Julii are back at the heart of Rome."

"Mother, I hope I won't disappoint you," said Quintus softly. "I'll do everything I can."

"I know that. Now it's time to celebrate."

Moments later, the family stepped out of their courtyard followed by six male slaves. A small crowd was waiting in the alley to wave Quintus off.

"Well done, son!"

"Good luck!"

"It's too bad your father's not here to see this," murmured Aurelia as they slowly processed towards the centre of the city, "and it's shaming that we can't muster more than six slaves, but at least this afternoon we're joining General Marius. The other families will have to take note of that."

After a long stately parade through Rome's main avenues, they reached the Liber Temple and Aurelia sent the slaves home. The family climbed the steps of the ancient stone building perched on the highest of the city's seven hills and, after prayers and a blessing, a notary slave added Quintus's name to the list of Roman citizens with an impressive peacock quill.

"Congratulations, sir. How are you celebrating?"

"We're off to the games now," said Quintus happily.

"I hope you have fun. It's a big day. Enjoy it."

"Do you have an invitation?" asked a short, bearded soldier when Aurelia, Quintus and Gaius finally reached the point where the crowded lane entered the Forum.

"Of course," answered Aurelia haughtily. "I am General Marius's sister-in-law and these are his nephews. We are his guests."

The centurion bowed and beckoned them through the cordon. "You must be the Julii family. We've been asked to look out for you. Come with me."

Rome's grand central square had been converted into an arena for the day. In the middle was a large circle of sand. This was surrounded by several lines of plush seats and behind that row upon row of packed wooden benches. Hazy blue smoke from charcoal braziers filled the place with the delicious smell of roasting spiced meat. In one corner crates were piled high with spitting jaguars, snarling leopards and skinny lions with moulting manes. Beyond that was an iron cage of men dressed in loincloths – the gladiators, the main entertainment of the day.

The soldier led the Julii family down an aisle between the cheap seats where each bench heaved with six or seven people rammed into a space only comfortable for four. Finally they reached a silk cord. Beyond this were three rows of spacious lacquered wooden chairs lined with scarlet cushions. Instead of cramming in, the grander families of Rome moved easily from one seat to the next, greeting family and friends.

The soldier pulled the rope aside and pointed ahead. Gaius couldn't believe it; they were to be seated in the front row. He'd only been to the games once before – two years ago when his father was last home – but then their seats had been so far back that he'd spent most of the afternoon trying to find a gap to peer through. But this time nothing would block his view.

"Isn't this fantastic?" he whispered to Quintus, who grinned back at him.

"Here are your places," said the soldier. "Madame, the general requested that you sit next to him."

Aurelia couldn't hide her delight. She turned this way and that so everyone in the crowd could see that she was seated in the place of honour. Only once she had smoothed every last pleat of her blue silk toga did she settle down in her chair.

"Excuse me, madam," said an olive-skinned slave with dark narrow eyes and a pea-sized brown mole on one cheek. He spoke perfect Latin but with a heavy accent. "General Marius has instructed me to look after you and your family this afternoon. Here are blankets to keep you warm. Can I bring you anything to eat?"

Although the words were polite enough, there was something distinctly insolent about their delivery. Slaves were supposed to be submissive and docile but this man was almost rude.

Aurelia stared at him disdainfully as she wrapped a striped cover around her legs. "Aren't you the young slave I bought for General Marius last week?"

"I am. That's why my master told me to serve you today … to show his gratitude."

"Then you'd better watch your tone, or he'll hardly be thanking me for long. Your sister seems much more obliging. Now, what is there to eat?"

"Stuffed dates, ham, pomegranates, figs, skewers of beef and roasted dormouse."

The slave spoke in the same surly manner but this time Aurelia chose to ignore it. She wanted to have fun, not deal with his truculence.

"We'll have everything and a jug of wine." She smiled at Quintus. "It'll be army porridge for you from tomorrow so make the most of it."

The slave disappeared off in the direction of the braziers. Moments later a ram's horn echoed around the Forum.

"Your host, General Marius," announced a soldier to a deafening cheer.

Into the square walked a tall man in a scarlet cape and a leather breastplate studded with bronze.

Although Gaius had worn Marius's charm for all of his eleven years, he hardly knew his famous uncle, as the general had retired to his lavish country estate by the sea many years ago. "Marius wasn't born an aristocrat," his mother often said, "but we forgive him for when barbarians came marauding towards Rome, he saved the city and he was rewarded by being elected Consul six times."

The crowd cheered ecstatically, but Gaius was disappointed by Marius's sagging knees and snow-white hair. For all the pomp and excitement surrounding him, the general looked old and worn.

A line of priests entered the sandy arena as the ancient soldier declared in a gruff voice, "Romans, the games will begin!" Then he sat down and turned to Gaius's mother.

"Aurelia, you haven't changed a bit. Are you finding things to your liking?"

"Everything is delightful, except that slave I sent you. I apologize. I thought he would be pleasanter than that."

Marius smiled, revealing long chalky teeth. "Don't worry. I'll soon have any insolence knocked out of him and then I plan to pass him on to my sister. It was generous of you but I have too many slaves and she too few. Now introduce me to your sons. They've grown so much, I hardly recognize them."

Aurelia smiled graciously. "This is Quintus and that's Gaius."

"And it's Quintus who's become a citizen today, I hear," said Marius approvingly. "Congratulations. Now if you don't mind, boys, I need a word with your mother."

Gaius and Quintus stood up and wandered down the

row of seats. The priests were parading around the arena's sand, wafting incense and singing prayers, taking forever to bless the square. Like the fidgeting crowd, Gaius was soon bored so he headed back to his seat where he was surprised to hear his mother say sharply, "Marius, it's Sulpicius stirring up trouble that worries me."

"You're right to be concerned," the general replied. "This business with Sulpicius and Sulla could end in war. They hate each other."

Sulla? Gaius was surprised. *Wasn't Sulla Consul of Rome? And wasn't Sulpicius a Roman senator who occasionally visited when his father was on leave?*

Just then a pomegranate flew over their heads and rolled across the sand.

Marius patted Aurelia's hand.

"Apologies, my dear, the crowd is getting restless and I must get on with the ceremony. But never forget Sulla hates our family, so be careful."

He got to his feet and clapped his hands, and moments later two brawny men, one six inches taller than the other, entered the arena. The taller gladiator carried a net in one hand and a trident in the other. The shorter one wore a silver helmet that covered his face and was armed with a shield and dagger. For no particular reason, Gaius decided he wanted the shorter one to win.

"We who are about to die salute you," shouted the gladiators in unison.

Gaius was mesmerized. Who would attack first? The

men began circling each other, taut with concentration, and then suddenly the taller man jabbed with his trident. There was a clash of steel and then the smaller man's dagger caught his opponent's thigh, leaving a thin streak of blood. Gaius cheered wildly. His man had the advantage.

"Master, your food." It was the slave, holding out a plate, but Gaius ignored him. He didn't want to miss a thing.

The injured man was now staggering around. The cut was deeper than it looked but instead of going in for the kill, the gladiator Gaius had chosen hesitated. Suddenly his rival threw the net, catching him off guard, and his helmet rolled across the sand as he fell to the ground trapped in the wire mesh.

"Now you can give me some figs," said Gaius, annoyed the contest was over so quickly, but the slave did not respond.

"I said, figs," said Gaius irritably, but the slave wasn't listening. Instead he was staring at the defeated gladiator.

"Who is he?" Gaius asked.

"He's my brother," the slave mumbled. "We were captured together."

By now the beaten gladiator was wrapped in the net as tightly as a fly in a spider's web and General Marius was walking towards the centre of the ring.

"Today my nephew became a citizen of Rome and tomorrow he joins his father's legion in the east," he announced. "To celebrate, he will have the privilege of deciding this man's fate. Quintus Julius Caesar, come here."

Aurelia beamed. Her son was to be at the centre of the first drama. The last time Gaius had been to the games he had loved the excitement of this moment, but this time the slave's misery was spoiling it.

"It's the slave's brother. Why not spare him?" he hissed as Quintus stood up, flushed with delight.

"What's it to be?" asked Marius when Quintus reached the centre of the arena.

Gaius held his index finger to his thumb but all around people were booing with thumbs down. "He's useless," they shouted. "He doesn't deserve mercy."

"Quintus, have you made up your mind?" asked the general.

Perhaps he didn't hear me, thought Gaius, so he stood up and shouted at his brother, "Spare him! Spare him!" but his voice was drowned out by the mob.

Quintus hesitated for a second and then to the delight of the crowd he theatrically raised his left thumb and turned it towards the ground. Immediately the victorious gladiator cut his opponent's throat with a dagger. The dying gladiator let out a spine-chilling yell as blood spilled across the white sand.

"What on earth are you doing?" whispered Aurelia, pulling Gaius back to his seat. "You're making a spectacle of yourself."

"I thought Quintus should save him," protested Gaius. "He's the brother of the slave you gave Uncle."

"A slave's troubles are beneath us. You must never take an interest."

Gaius sank back into his seat. Another set of gladiators fought and then another and another. He watched each clash but the fun had gone out of it and he was relieved when at last the arena was covered with splodges of blood, the games were over and they were saying their goodbyes.

"Thank you for coming, boys," said their host jovially. "Glad you enjoyed it."

"I'm not sure Gaius did," piped a voice.

It was a girl of around twelve years old, sitting on the far side of the general. She was fair-skinned, with blue eyes, high cheekbones and blond hair elaborately plaited in a style too grown up for her age.

Marius laughed.

"Allow me to introduce my niece. Atia, whatever are you talking about?"

The girl smirked. "I don't think Gaius has the stomach for blood. Didn't you notice? He wanted to spare that useless first gladiator."

Before Gaius could respond, Aurelia said firmly, "Marius, I can assure you no Julii is a coward. Now come along, boys. It is time we were getting home."

"Gaius! I told you!" his mother hissed once they'd reached the edge of the Forum and the crowd had thinned. "You'll never amount to a thing if you are weak. Thank the gods for Quintus. At least I have one son who'll bring me honour."

Perhaps she's right, Gaius thought sadly. Why had he let the feelings of an unknown slave bother him? And he'd done the same with Zoe. He was weak and cursed. How could he ever bring honour to his family?

6

EARLY the next morning Gaius helped Quintus mount a bony horse in the courtyard of their home. As he climbed on to his equally skinny mare he wished that he too were off to join the army, instead of just carrying his brother's luggage to camp. Once Quintus was gone the house would be so lonely and his brother would be away for months, just like the father they so rarely saw.

"Promise me you'll be careful," Aurelia begged her eldest son. "There could be bandits on the road, especially when you get further east."

"I won't be alone. There'll be a hundred men with me," Quintus replied happily.

"Still, I'll pray for you." She turned to Gaius. "Make sure you're back at the Equiline Gate by sunset. I don't want to have to pay one extra sestertii for the hire of these nags. They're a disgrace. If we could afford a stable of our own I'd beat any slave that let an animal get into this condition. They're bound to slow you down..."

"Mother, don't fret," said Quintus, pulling on his scarlet cape and fastening his bronze helmet. "Gaius will be back in time and don't worry about me. I shall be fine."

A slave did one last check, testing the knots, and then

the courtyard gates were thrown open and the boys waved goodbye and trotted off.

Nudging their way through the crowded alleys was frustrating but once they had passed through the city gate they made good progress along a cobbled road lined with fancy marble tombs. The sky was clear and there was a sharp frost on the ground. Gaius enjoyed the steady clip-clopping of his horse and was relieved to be away from his mother. Since yesterday's games all she had done was remind him of what a fool he'd been, and in front of General Marius.

It was midday when they reached a crossroads at the top of a hill. In the valley below were six bleached tents either side of a rocky stream.

"That's my camp," said Quintus. "I'll walk from here." He jumped down, handed Gaius his reins and began to untie the saddle bags.

"Are you sure?" asked Gaius. "It's a lot to carry."

"I'll manage. It's not far and I don't want you to be late for Mother. It'll only aggravate her." He smiled. "And somehow you seem to do enough of that."

"It's not my fault," Gaius protested.

"I know. It's only because she's worried."

"Why? Because we don't live on the Palatine Hill?"

"No, because trouble is brewing."

"You mean with Sulla?" asked Gaius, remembering the conversation he had overheard at the games.

"Yes. Since Sulla became Consul he's taken so many

bribes that many of the senators are saying he can't remain in office. Sulpicius loathes him the most and is demanding that he goes now. But Sulla won't go quietly. It's now such a mess that Marius has returned to Rome to see if he can sort things out."

"What can the general do?"

"It's too soon for him to stand as Consul again, but at tomorrow's elections he's going to try to persuade the people to vote for his ally, Cinna. He's hoping that Sulpicius and the other senators can then be persuaded to put up with Sulla for his last six months as Consul if they know a good man is following. Otherwise it could mean war."

"Between Romans?" Gaius was shocked. His tutor, Gnipo, had taught him that, while the barbarian tribes often fought among themselves, Romans were always united. This was how they had defeated every king that got in their way. "But we never turn on ourselves. We're too disciplined for that."

"Until now we have been, but things are changing." Quintus unfastened his last bag.

"What happens if there is war?"

"I don't know. It's never happened before."

A trumpet sounded in the valley below.

"I'd better go," said Quintus.

"Good luck," said Gaius.

"And to you. I have a feeling we might both need it."

* * *

Sadly Gaius watched his brother walk down the steep valley towards the cluster of tents. *Rome at war!* It was impossible to imagine. The city was so advanced. There was no other place in the world like it.

His horse pawed the ground impatiently, reminding Gaius that he should be heading home. He spurred his mare in the flank and tugged on the reins of Quintus's horse. "Come on. We can't be late."

The nags seemed to understand for they flattened their ears and sprang forward. Gaius's brown cloak flapped and his horse's straggly mane flicked his face but he did nothing to slow the pace. They overtook carts loaded with vegetables for the city's markets and slaves being marched from the ports. Much sooner than he'd expected he spotted the city walls and the tatty stables by the Equiline Gate. All of a sudden Gaius realized what a gift this was. It was well before sunset – the perfect time to find Tribune Rufus Agrippa and deliver Marta's message.

He paid the groom slave, and hurried across the Forum and along the busy Sacra Via until he reached a broad avenue lined with lavish mansions that curled uphill. He began to climb, passing a veiled woman dressed in the latest silks and several senators, their togas marked by a distinctive crimson stripe.

Gaius stopped a slave and asked for directions.

"The Agrippa family? You can't miss the house, master. It's the largest building on the Hill, right at the top, with yellow walls."

At last the avenue levelled out and there, on the opposite side of the road, was a high wall of perfectly smooth primrose plaster with a pair of magnificent carved wooden doors.

"I'm here to see Tribune Rufus Agrippa," Gaius announced to the guard.

"And who should I say is calling?"

Gaius stood up tall and straight, and tried to sound important. "I am Gaius Julius Caesar."

The man nodded, unimpressed. "Follow me."

They entered a small courtyard.

"Leave your sandals with her," said the guard, pointing at a kneeling slave girl, "and come this way."

Hastily Gaius untied his shoes and then crossed a magnificent atrium lined with gold pillars and marble statues. In the centre was a pond with a fountain carved in the shape of three diving dolphins.

"Wait there," said the guard, pointing to a study with red walls. "I'll let the master know you're here."

The study had a large cedar wood desk, a bronze standing lamp and a heavy chest. At home Gaius could always hear the babble of street traders in the crowded alleys outside, but this room was eerily silent.

"Not interrupting, am I?"

Gaius jumped. Only a foot away was a man of around twenty years with short, curly hair, a clean-shaven face dominated by a large nose, and a gleaming white toga. His disdainful look made Gaius feel awkward, as if he had been caught snooping.

"Not at all," he said quickly. "I have a message for Rufus Agrippa. May I ask if that is you, sir?"

"It is. Who's your message from?"

"Vestal Marta."

Immediately the tribune grabbed Gaius's arm, pulling him close.

"If you've spoken to Marta," he hissed, "then keep your voice down. When did you see her?"

Gaius was startled. "Two days ago, on Martis, at the Temple of Vesta."

"Why did she send a message with you?"

"I... I was there. And we're related," he mumbled. "I'm a Julii."

"A Julii?" Rufus was clutching Gaius's arm so tightly it hurt. "Then you are also related to my general, Marius. Well, what did she say?"

"She said to tell you, 'Meet at the steps of the Temple of Castor and Pollux at sunset, this Saturni.'"

"Nothing else?"

"No."

The tribune relaxed his grip. "Have you told anybody else about this?"

"No. Now please, can I go?"

"Yes," said Rufus. "But keep your mouth shut. I'll find out if you don't."

7

THE journey home from the Palatine Hill took longer than he thought it would and by the time Gaius got home it was dark. He opened the courtyard gate expecting his mother to pounce on him, demanding to know where he had been, but instead found the house strangely quiet.

After checking the study and Aurelia's bedroom, he poked his head into the cramped, smoky kitchen where Flora, the cook slave, lived and worked. He found her sitting on her camp bed stirring porridge in a blackened pot.

"There you are, master. After some supper, I suppose?"

"Actually I was looking for Mother."

"She's gone and she won't be back until dusk tomorrow, leaving me with not a sestertii to run the household." Flora ladled out some porridge and passed it over to him. "But she left instructions – you're to stay home until she returns."

"But the elections are tomorrow," protested Gaius. "I want to go."

"That's as may be, master, but those are her orders. Now eat that up before it gets cold."

Gaius perched on a stool next to the brick hearth.

"Where's she gone?"

"That uncle of yours spooked her with his tales of war. She's looking for somewhere to stay outside the city if things get difficult."

"Are you scared?"

Flora rolled her eyes. "Wars are for masters; they make no difference to slaves. All I want is my freedom, although around here that seems too much to ask for after years of good labour."

"I'm sure Mother will let you go one day," said Gaius, "once Zoe has learned what to do in the kitchen."

"'One day' will be too late, master. My village is high in the Atlas Mountains and an old woman can't make the journey alone. Now just look at this fire. Zoe!"

The slave appeared at the door. It was the first time Gaius had seen her since he'd discovered her hiding behind his mother's chest. She was plainer than he remembered, with ugly tufts of hair.

"Zoe, I've told you a hundred times," complained Flora, "this fire must never go out. It brings bad luck."

"Is the wood not in the right place?" The girl frowned, pointing at a pile of timber.

"Yes, but you must keep putting logs on. When you've done that, sweep the floor and get the dough ready for the morning. I'm tired."

Zoe's shoulders drooped as Flora heaved herself under the camp bed's rumpled blankets. Gaius finished up his porridge. After his long day he too was tired and couldn't wait to go to bed.

* * *

Early the next morning Gaius was woken by loud noises coming from the alley beneath his window. Pulling his linen sheet around his shoulders, he pushed open the shutters, letting in a draught of cold air. It was the first day of the month of Januarius and thousands of people were heading towards the Sanqualis Gate, the quickest way out to the Field of Mars, where the annual election for Consul was to be held as it had been held each New Year's Day for centuries.

Young boys clung to their fathers' hands, trotting along excitedly. Gaius was envious. He loved the elections – the speeches from the different candidates' pens and then the drama of the count, particularly if it was close. Every citizen of the Republic was entitled to vote and many travelled miles from the provinces just to take part. But here he was, in Rome, unable to go and watch.

Morosely he dressed himself in his usual blue tunic, leg wrappings and woollen cape and sat down to a lonely breakfast of bread and goat's cheese. The morning stretched ahead of him and after wandering aimlessly around the villa, he picked up his wax tablet and stylus. At least he could finish the Greek to Latin translation that Gnipo had set him. But his heart wasn't in it and he was continually distracted by shouts of excitement from outside.

After what felt like an age he had only managed to translate two sentences but at least the lane outside was quieter. Everyone must have left the city by now. Suddenly Gaius could stand it no longer. What could be the harm in him going too? Flora never left the kitchen so she wouldn't notice and none of the other slaves would dare say a word to his mother.

He crept across the courtyard, tied on his sandals and slipped outside. The alley was deserted. Even the beggars had abandoned their corners and the shops were shuttered up for the day.

Gaius began to walk quickly, eager to catch up with the early morning crowd, but he had only taken a few paces when someone shouted, "Hey!" He turned around and saw a boy about his age hurrying towards him. He had shaggy black shoulder-length hair and a round face, and was dressed almost identically to Gaius in a blue tunic, leggings and a brown cape.

"Are you going to the elections?" the boy asked breathlessly. "My name is Alexander Theopolis. My father and I moved here last week from Ostia."

Gaius remembered a cart piled precariously high with furniture and sacks causing havoc in the narrow lane.

"My father's Greek so he's not allowed to vote," the boy continued. "I tried to persuade him to take me anyway, but he wouldn't. Do you mind if I join you? I don't know the way and I don't want to go alone."

The boy seemed friendly enough so Gaius said, "Of course. If we hurry, we might even get there in time for the vote."

* * *

The Field of Mars was a wide meadow, sandwiched between the city walls and the River Tiber. Usually it was a lonely place, used for military exercises and target practice, but by the time Gaius and Alexander arrived it was teeming with people. Children, women and slaves were milling around while the men separated into several vast wooden pens. Each candidate had erected a fenced-off compound for their supporters. Three of the pens had only a couple of hundred men inside, but one was so packed they were spilling out, waving their hands, trying to catch the attention of frazzled soldiers in scarlet uniforms doing the count.

"The vote must be almost finished," said Gaius. He turned to the nearest woman. "Excuse me, madam, do you know who's won?"

"I've heard it's Cinna. Sulla will be furious because that's General Marius's candidate and not his own."

The soldiers must have completed their count for suddenly the men surged out of their pens towards a wooden platform erected in the middle of the muddy field where Sulla would announce the results.

"Let's get as close to the stage as we can," said Gaius, tugging Alexander's sleeve.

By squeezing their way through gaps in the crowd, they managed to work their way to the front, where they were surrounded by people all speculating as to what might happen next.

"The Consul's taking his time. Do you think he'll allow the result to stand?"

"He's got no choice."

"But he's a wild one with a terrible temper. They say he never likes to be crossed."

"And he's rich enough to buy half the Roman army. He won't be short of soldiers if he chooses to fight."

Time passed and still there was no sign of the Consul. Drizzle began to fall from the grey sky and the crowd became impatient.

"He's trying to fix the result."

"I don't know why we elected him last year. I'm telling you, there's going to be trouble."

At last, just when several members of the crowd were starting to boo, a red-haired man with a ruddy face and a barrel of a stomach climbed on to the stage. He wore a cloak heavily embroidered with gold and silver thread, his cheeks were clumsily rouged and a huge pearl pendant dangled over his ample belly. Most Roman men dressed austerely in a simple toga and sandals but Sulla was famous for his flashy displays of wealth. Even his shoes were studded with nuggets of gold.

The man sauntered across the platform and held up his hands, demanding silence.

"Citizens, it has been an honour to serve as your Consul for the past six months," he boomed. "Rome faces many dangers. There are rebels in the south and not enough soldiers to guard the city but I have always done my best to keep you safe." He grimaced. "It is now my duty to tell you that in six months' time, at the end of the month of Quintillis, Cinna is your choice to take over this heavy responsibility. He will become Consul and then we shall see how well he does. It is easy to look like a leader, but not so easy to rule..."

"It doesn't sound like he's going to fight the result after all," Gaius heard someone say.

"No. It looks like General Marius has pulled off another miracle. Rome would be lost without him. That's why we chose him to be our Consul six times all those years ago."

Just then Alexander said, "Gaius, I should get back before Father starts to worry."

Gaius glanced at the sky. The sun was hidden by clouds but he could see that it was well past its zenith. He too should be getting home.

"I'll come with you," he said, and once more they jostled their way through the crowd.

"Why did you move from Ostia?" Gaius asked once they were strolling along the emptier road back towards the city.

"I want to be an engineer. A friend of Father's is working on the city's new aqueduct. A month ago he offered to let me study with him. Luckily, Father was planning to set up as a doctor here too."

"Is it just the two of you?"

"No. Mother is packing the last of our things. She'll join us in a couple of months but a priest told Father he should start his new business at the beginning of the year."

"Do you work on the aqueduct all day?"

"Just in the mornings. I'm using the afternoons to learn my way around Rome. There are so many amazing things to see."

The more Alexander spoke, the more Gaius liked him, so he asked, "Have you visited the baths yet?"

"No."

"Then come with me tomorrow afternoon. You'll be impressed."

By now they had reached Rome's walls and were standing in a long queue waiting to pass through the gate.

"What's the hold-up?" someone ahead asked.

"Some slaves have escaped so the soldiers are checking everyone in and out."

The taller of the two men immediately in front of Alexander and Gaius shrugged. "We could be here for a while. I'm glad we left early as this queue will only get worse and the election didn't go as I expected."

"What do you mean?" asked his companion.

"I reckon General Marius missed a chance."

At the mention of his uncle's name Gaius began to pay more attention.

"How?"

"When he was a boy," the tall man explained, "Marius found a bird's nest with seven eggs in the hem of his cloak. His parents worried it was an ill omen but a priest convinced them that it meant he would be voted Consul seven times – once for each egg. When I heard he'd returned to Rome I was certain he'd be elected this year for the seventh time. He's almost seventy. If it doesn't happen soon, it will never happen."

Seven eggs! Suddenly Gaius realized this idle chatter was the key to his riddle. Vestal Fulvia Pollo had said, 'The Julii will rise when the last egg hatches.' And Marta had told him that the seventh egg was the last egg... The prophesy must be about Marius!

"I'll race you home," he said to Alexander once they were finally through the city gate. He was sure his mother would be delighted that he had solved the puzzle. But he was wrong; she was furious.

8

AS soon as Gaius arrived home he went straight to his mother's room. He found her sitting at her dressing table wiping off make-up with a strip of oiled linen.

"Where have you been?" she asked crossly. "Didn't Flora tell you not to leave the villa?"

"I know I shouldn't have, but I have good news!" Eagerly Gaius told her all about the men he'd overheard and how the riddle must mean that once Marius was elected Consul for a seventh time the Julii would see better days. But far from congratulating him for his cleverness, Aurelia flushed with rage.

"How dare you suggest such a thing!" His mother threw down a cloth smudged with scarlet lipstick. "Don't link our fortunes to that prophesy!"

"Why?"

"Because Marius will never be elected Consul again. He's far too old. Now leave! I'm exhausted. And next time, do as I say or there'll be trouble!"

That night Gaius slept fitfully. Despite his mother's fury, he was still convinced that he was right about the vestal's riddle. He dreamed of grotesque versions of Marius, Sulla and his mother at a strange election where nothing ever got decided and somehow he was to blame, so he was relieved when he saw the first grey light of dawn through the cracks in his shutters.

He dressed, ate breakfast, and then walked through the misty alleys to his tutor's apartment.

"Gnipo," he said once lessons were over, "is it possible that General Marius could be elected Consul once more?"

His tutor warmed his bony fingers by the glowing coals. "It's unlikely ... but then so was serving six times."

"Why?"

"Under Roman law a Consul is elected for twelve months and then cannot seek re-election for at least ten years. The system is designed to stop any one man from becoming too powerful."

"Then how did Marius become Consul six times?"

The old tutor smiled. "Ah, there's a story. Years ago, just after he was voted Consul for the first time, tribes from Germania attacked Rome. Marius is a fine general and crushed them easily, but three years later more barbarians came and the new Consul struggled. In desperation the senators begged Marius to return but he refused, knowing it was against the law. So the senators changed the law and Marius ruled for the next five years. During that time he defeated the Germanic tribes and saved the city. Once the job was done, the law was changed back again and he retired to his country estate in glory."

"When was he last Consul?"

"Let me see ... it would have been eight years ago."

"So he could be elected in two years' time."

"Of course, if the gods will it." Gnipo sounded doubtful. "But there are other, younger men. It would take a real emergency for Rome to turn back to General Marius."

Gaius was dejected. The riddle seemed to promise something that was impossible. Why would the gods play such a trick?

"Shouldn't you be getting home instead of worrying about the ambitions of old men?" asked Gnipo kindly.

"How late is it?" asked Gaius.

The tutor pushed open a shutter, looking for the sun. "Around midday."

Suddenly Gaius remembered that he'd promised to show Alexander the city's grandest baths. He scooped his wax tablet and stylus into his satchel.

"Thank you, Gnipo. I'll see you tomorrow."

"How was your morning?" Gaius asked Alexander as they jogged towards the bathhouse.

"Amazing. I was actually inside an aqueduct helping with measurements. The engineers have to be so precise. The water travels miles from a spring in the mountain but must only drop two inches every hundred yards."

At last they reached a broad paved square lined with grand colonnaded buildings. On the far side was the red and green stone entrance of the public bathhouse, the largest in Rome, renowned for its lavish gym, sauna, steam rooms and endless supply of warm water.

They climbed its marble steps and then Petronius, a slave with an enormous tummy, a round face and a beaming smile said, "Welcome, master, and who are you with today?"

"This is Alexander Theopolis." Gaius handed over a copper coin. "It's his first time at the baths."

"Then I hope he enjoys his visit. Vetus will look after you both this afternoon."

A young slave boy stepped forward.

"Will you need the gymnasium, masters?"

"No. We worked up a sweat running here."

"Very good. Then come this way."

Vetus led them across a courtyard decorated with opulent statues and lavish mosaics of fish, dolphins, squid, whales and the determined face of Neptune, god of the sea. Every detail, even the fishes' scales and the tips of Neptune's silver trident, was picked out in thousands of tiny brightly coloured squares.

"None of Ostia's baths compares with this," said Alexander, stopping to gaze at a particularly fine mosaic of a leaping salmon.

"This is nothing," said Gaius. "Just wait till you see the pool."

In the heated changing room they handed Vetus their clothes, smeared themselves in olive oil, and each took a gown and some wooden clogs from a large pile in the centre of the chamber.

Vetus led them to a room that was so hot each breath burnt the back of their throats and their faces were soon beetroot red.

"I won't take long," said the slave, running a stirgil over their arms, legs and torso, scraping away any dirt with the curved metal tool; and then, to their relief, they left the sweltering room behind and entered the tepidarium. This was a vast marble chamber with an arched ceiling thirty feet high and an enormous swimming pool. Its edge was lined with a carved stone bench and shallow steps led into the aquamarine water. In the far corner of the pool a couple of rotund men were lazily floating about, but otherwise Alexander and Gaius had the place to themselves.

"What do you think?" asked Gaius.

"It's amazing. I've never seen anything like it." Alexander left his robe and clogs on the side, climbed down the steps and dipped a toe in the water. "I wonder how they keep it so warm. There must be a furnace somewhere."

Alexander gazed around the room and quickly spotted several lead pipes on the far side of the pool near to where steaming water was spurting from the mouth of a stone lion. "It'll be at that end."

They swam across the pool and Alexander pressed his ear against the wall. "Listen – you can hear it. It must be huge."

Gaius leaned closer and heard a rushing sound, like

wind, and the bricks were warm.

"That's hot air," explained Alexander.

"Everything all right, master?"

Petronius was standing at the water's edge, his hands resting on his ample belly, looking perplexed by the two boys listening intently to the wall.

"Alexander wants to be an engineer," explained Gaius. "We're trying to hear the furnace."

The slave grinned. "An engineer, eh? Then you're a man after my own heart. Would you like me to show you the heating system?"

"Yes, please," Alexander answered enthusiastically.

They climbed out of the pool, fetched their robes and clogs, and met Petronius by a small unobtrusive door in the corner of the tepidarium. This led to a narrow cement and brick corridor lined with shelves. Each shelf was covered with hundreds of neatly arranged jars and flasks of oils, unguents and creams. Halfway along they passed one jar fractionally out of line with the rest and Petronius tutted and pushed it back into place before waddling on.

"Now this is where the real action happens," he said, leading them at last into a large chamber.

The room had a ceiling as high as the tepidarium and from it hung three gigantic black kettles. Below each kettle were huge fires, continually stoked by slaves.

"It's baking in here," said Gaius. "I don't know how the slaves can stand it."

Petronius wiped several drips of sweat from his chin.

"They can't for long. They work shifts – a morning or an afternoon at the most, and then even the toughest need to rest."

Gaius mopped his own brow with the sleeve of his robe. "Why not open a window? It's so hot."

"It has to be, master," said Petronius. "The hot air is captured and circulates under the bathhouse floors to keep them warm, and the kettles heat the water you bathe in. The flames burn day and night so nothing is ever allowed to cool."

"Thank you for showing us around," said Alexander, with eyes like saucers. "I've never seen anything like it."

"Glad to be of service," said Petronius. "Now we should be getting back. I've other areas to check up on. If I don't keep an eye on the place it soon falls into rack and ruin."

He hurried across the chamber, wheezing a little as he went, and passed through another door. Gaius was relieved to be away from the searing heat, but moments later they were hit by a hideous sulphurous smell.

"What's that?" he asked, covering his nose.

"I should have warned you, master. Rome's main sewer runs right under here."

"It smells disgusting!"

Petronius smiled. "I know it's unpleasant, master, but just imagine Rome without it. Half a million people doing their business every day! The city would be a cesspit."

"And it's an amazing feat of engineering," added Alexander. "I've heard it's the first of its kind and it flushes directly into the River Tiber."

"That's right, just by the bridge. And if it ever needs repairs, slaves climb through here to do them." Petronius pointed to a wooden door so small it looked more like a cupboard. "The tunnel is big enough for a man to walk through. Now come this way."

He led them down another passage. "This takes us to the main entrance. Turn left and you'll get to the pool. I must check on the gym."

A little further on, the boys opened a door and found themselves back in the bathhouse's grand, marble entrance hall.

"Let's go to the tepidarium," said Gaius. "After that furnace I need a swim."

But they were only halfway across the hall when someone shouted his name. He turned, and with a sinking heart, recognized Rufus Agrippa.

"You go on, Alexander," he said. "I won't be long."

"I've been looking for you," Rufus said accusingly, as soon as Gaius was in earshot. "You must deliver this note to Marta today."

He pressed a small tightly wrapped scroll into Gaius's hand.

"But I'm not going to the temple."

"Then find a reason to."

"I don't know what you and Marta are up to," Gaius said irritably, "but I'm not getting involved."

"You're already involved. And if you don't do as I say, by

dawn the whole of Rome will hear of that curse of yours. Just think what that will do to the reputation of the Julii."

Gaius couldn't believe his ears. The only people who knew of his curse were his mother, Flora and Fulvia Pollo, who would never speak of anything the gods had told her. Then, with a sickening feeling, he remembered – Zoe! She'd promised never to tell anyone, but you could never trust a new slave. He should have known!

"But no one will know," continued the tribune, "if this is delivered tonight."

He pressed the scroll into Gaius's hand once more and this time Gaius took it. Somehow he had to find a way of returning to the Temple of Vesta.

9

BY the time Gaius got home the sun was low in the sky. There wasn't much time to take Rufus Agrippa's wretched scroll to Marta, but there was something else he had to sort out first.

He looked in the dining room and was surprised to see Corax, a weary old slave who did odd jobs around the villa, setting the table.

"Where's Zoe?" he asked.

"You haven't heard, master?" the man answered. "She's run away."

Gaius couldn't believe it. Slaves hardly ever ran away; the punishment was too great. If they were caught, they were crucified or forced to become gladiators.

"When did this happen?" he asked.

"This afternoon, master. It's put Flora in a terrible mood. She's had to go to the baker herself to fetch bread for supper."

Gaius didn't care about Flora but hearing that for once she was out of the kitchen gave him an idea.

"I'll fetch the wine," he said.

Corax was shocked. "No need, master. I'll do it."

"No. You go to all the city gates and tell them that we

have a runaway and make sure you give a good description of Zoe. I want her back by morning."

Once Corax had left Gaius headed for the kitchen. It was a poky room, the walls stained by years of black smoke. In one corner was Flora's camp bed and next to that was a brick grate where a large pot of stew was gently bubbling. Gaius crossed to a wall of shelves cluttered with jars and bottles of honey, salted olives, dried fish, olive oil and wine. He picked up a bottle of wine, took it over to the grate and deliberately smashed it down on the stone hearth. The pottery flagon broke into a thousand pieces and red wine ran everywhere.

"Master, what happened!" Flora was standing in the doorway holding a couple of loaves.

"I tripped," Gaius fibbed. "I thought I'd help but the bottle was too heavy."

Flora dumped the bread on the camp bed. "Quick, give me the bellows!" She knelt down and tried pumping air onto the damp logs but it was hopeless.

"What will your mother say!" she cried, wringing her gnarled hands. "She's got guests coming and the food will get cold."

"Couldn't we light a torch from a neighbour's fire, just this once?" Gaius asked, knowing Flora would never agree.

"No. The flame must come from the Temple of Vesta's sacred fire. The mistress insists upon it."

"Then I'll go," said Gaius. "It was my fault."

Flora handed him an unlit torch smeared with sticky black tar. "Thank you, master. Be as quick as you can."

By the time Gaius reached the Forum the sky was dark and the traders were packing up their stalls for the night. On the rostrum a man was addressing a growing crowd. He was middle-aged with a heavy, broken nose and a large belly that even his flowing toga couldn't hide. It was Sulpicius, one of the leading senators in the city, and a sworn enemy of Sulla.

"The Consul is not to be trusted," he was shouting as Gaius walked past. "Sulla's stealing all Rome's gold."

"At least Sulla gets things done," someone shouted back.

"Only for himself," Sulpicius sneered. "And do you really believe he will step aside when it's no longer his turn to rule?"

Another voice in the swelling crowd began to heckle. Gaius hurried on. It looked like trouble was brewing; he was determined to deliver Rufus's scroll to Marta and get home as soon as he could.

Swiftly he climbed the steps of the vestals' palace.

"If you're here for a light from the fire," said the guard, keeping one eye on the boisterous crowd, "go to the back of the temple."

Gaius joined a long queue.

I wish they'd hurry," muttered a woman in front of him. "That crowd's going to get ugly, especially after they've had a few drinks."

Grumbling and whining, the people in the queue shuffled slowly towards a narrow arched entrance. Several yards beyond that was another doorway from which a steady stream of people emerged with burning torches.

"Follow me, master," said a portly slave when Gaius finally reached the doorway of the temple.

He entered a circular hall with black, curved marble walls, four cedar doors and a domed ceiling. The room could have been dark and austere, but the walls were covered with hundreds of lanterns, their flames reflected in the polished stone. The place was a hive of activity, with slaves scurrying about collecting and returning torches to their weary owners but, disappointingly for Gaius, there was not a vestal to be seen.

"I need to see a priestess," he said to the slave who had shown him in. "Where are they?"

"In their palace, master." The slave gestured to a door down the hall. "They retire at nightfall. Now wait here while I light your torch."

I've been so stupid, Gaius thought. *Why did I think I'd find Marta here? I must get into the palace.*

He studied the circular hall once more. Apart from the hurrying slaves, people were milling around, waiting for their torches. Some sat on benches, others gossiped, but no one was paying him any attention. Slowly he crossed to the door the slave had pointed out. He looked around one last time, tried the handle and then slipped through, grabbing one of the lanterns as he went.

He found himself in a narrow corridor with a dank, unpleasant smell. It was dark and he was glad of his lantern. His heart pounded. What was he doing? If he were discovered, he couldn't imagine what the punishment would be. *But what's the alternative?* Gaius asked himself. *Rufus has given me no choice.* He took several deep breaths, held up his torch and tiptoed forward.

He must have taken more than two hundred paces before he came to a flight of steps. He swallowed nervously and then began to climb, counting as he went...one, two, three ... twenty stairs and then, at last, a door. He put the lamp on the floor and opened it just an inch. Ahead was a shadowy hall with more black marble walls, but this one had a red stripe across the ceiling. Thank the gods! He'd done it! He was in the very room where Fulvia Pollo had left him while she sacrificed the lamb. Marta couldn't be far away. But the question was, where?

He crept across the hall, looking for any clue as to which way to go next and then heard footsteps. Quickly he ducked behind a marble column.

"Who's there?"

Cautiously Gaius peeked out and saw the back of a girl in the flowing white robes of a vestal. She was peering this way and that, convinced she'd heard something. She turned and immediately Gaius recognized her striking blue eyes.

He couldn't believe his good fortune. It was Marta!

"It's me," he whispered. "Gaius Julius Caesar."

Marta's face was ashen and her eyes were wide with fright.

"What on earth are you doing here? It's much too dangerous."

"Tribune Rufus Agrippa's orders." Gaius pulled the scroll from his linen satchel and thrust it into her hand. "He told me to give you this. But from now on you'll both have to find another messenger. I'm not doing this any more."

With trembling hands Marta unrolled the grubby spool and quickly read it.

"You won't need to," she said. "It's done."

"What's done?"

"The less you know the better. Now let me get you out of here before you get us both killed. How did you get in?"

Quickly Gaius explained.

"Then you must go back that way." She took him to the door and bundled him through. Keeping one hand on the rough stone Gaius shuffled gingerly forward. Soon his toes curled around the edge of a step. Carefully he climbed down the first and then the second. On and on he went. Six ... seven ... eight steps. He couldn't wait to be away from this place. *Only five more to go*, he told himself. And then, from out of the darkness, stepped a shadowy figure.

"Good evening, Gaius Julius Caesar. What are you doing here?"

It was Vestal Fulvia Pollo, the last person he wanted to meet.

10

"I SAID, what are you doing here?" The old vestal's lips were tight with irritation. "No one is allowed in here without my permission. Are you seeing one of my girls?"

Gaius blushed. "Of course not!"

"Do you know what happens to them if they're caught alone with men? They're buried alive in a sealed pit. It takes a long time for them to die." Fulvia's eyes brightened gruesomely. "The thirst gets them in the end. It's a horrible way to go. So if there's a girl in here that you're sweet on, it's kinder to leave her alone."

"There isn't a girl, I swear."

"Then why are you here? Tell me!"

Gaius said nothing. Suddenly, before he had a chance to stop her, Fulvia grabbed the thong around his neck and shook it.

"My charm!" he protested, as his bulla fell from the pouch.

"I'll keep it until you tell me what you were doing here, so don't leave it too long. Remember, without it, you can't become a man."

She marched up the steps towards the vestals' palace leaving him once more in semi-darkness. Gaius felt sick.

He'd worn the charm since he was nine days old and he needed it to ward off evil spirits. And then he thought of his mother. If she knew it was gone, she would go out of her mind with worry.

Miserably he felt his way along the corridor. When he reached the temple hallway he found the squat slave waiting for him. Asking no questions, the slave held out the burning torch.

Gaius was relieved to get away from the place but he'd forgotten about the crowd in the Forum. It now covered half the square and Sulpicius was at its centre leading a chant of, "Sulla must go! Sulla must go!"

This could turn into a riot at any moment, thought Gaius. *I've got to get out of here.*

But it was too late. As he drew level with the rostrum, someone threw a rock. Though it narrowly missed Sulpicius, it acted like a spark – suddenly stones were flying everywhere. One whistled past Gaius's ear. He had to escape, but how? Soldiers were now pouring into the square, blocking the narrow alleys. They must be Sulla's men. As another missile smashed to the ground just inches away from him, he sprinted for the safety of the nearest building – the immense Temple of Castor and Pollux. He ran up its shallow marble steps three at a time heading for the massive bronze doors at the back of the portico where several other people were sheltering.

"What's going on?" he asked a priest in a long black gown and pointed hat.

"Sulpicius has been stirring up trouble all afternoon. He's picking a fight with the Consul and now he's got one."

Just then there was a tremendous smack on the temple's walls and a rock cracked the marble.

"Come! Quick!" shouted the priest, pushing them into a vast chamber with a huge statue of Jupiter at its centre and several altars covered in gold and jewels. He peered between a narrow gap in the bronze doors.

"What's happening?" quivered an old lady.

"It's hard to see, but I think Sulla's men are caught in this corner of the Forum. If they're not careful, they'll be trapped."

"Then shouldn't we leave before it gets worse?"

"It's too dangerous. It's mayhem out there."

Just then the noise grew louder and suddenly the temple doors were forced open. In ran a group of soldiers, several with ugly cuts on their faces and arms.

"Gentlemen! Gentlemen! Calm yourselves! This is a sacred place," protested the priest.

"Never mind that. Bar the door!" a large man shouted. He was dressed in a silk cape trimmed with silver and had rouged cheeks, grey eyes, and ginger, almost girlish, curls. To his horror Gaius realized it was Sulla.

"I said lock the door, you idiot! Sulpicius and his men are not far behind!"

With shaking hands, the priest lowered a wooden beam.

"It won't hold them back for long, sir," said a tall soldier.

"Is there another way out?" Sulla barked at the priest.

"No."

The old woman began to whimper.

"Silence!" snapped the Consul. He turned back to the tall soldier. "Officer, what do you suggest?"

"General Marius is the only man in Rome that Sulpicius respects. He alone could stop him from attacking you. You must get a message to the general."

"And how am I going to do that?" asked Sulla sarcastically, waving a podgy hand covered in rings. "Send a dove?"

Just then there was a loud bang on the door.

"This is Sulpicius," called a gruff voice. "You are surrounded. Give yourself up, Sulla, and spare the others."

"Never," roared the Consul, trembling with rage.

"You can't win. For once, do the honourable thing."

"I'd rather burn this place down and go with it than surrender to a fool like you!" shouted the incensed Consul. "I'm Sulla, do you hear?" And he lunged for Gaius's torch.

Gaius was terrified, but he wouldn't let go of the flame. He wasn't going to help this madman kill them all.

"Give it to me!" ordered Sulla. "How dare you defy me? What's your name?"

"Gaius Julius Caesar."

The Consul's eyes narrowed.

"General Marius's nephew?"

"Yes."

"Then the gods are with me," smiled the Consul. "I've found my ticket out of here."

11

SULPICIUS hammered on the door. "Sulla, will you surrender?"

The Consul grabbed Gaius and shouted through a crack in the door, "No. Take me to Marius."

"And why would I do that?"

"Because I have his nephew and the general won't thank you if he's killed."

There was a long pause. "Show me the boy."

Sulla drew his sword and then shoved Gaius outside with the blade at his neck. "Shall we go?" he said to the senator with a sour smile.

The three of them walked solemnly across the Forum and then up the Palatine Hill. Along the route the citizens of Rome stared apprehensively as they passed and all the time Gaius could feel the point of Sulla's sword grazing the top of his neck. One wrong move and he could be fatally wounded. He was relieved when they finally arrived at Marius's grand villa. Messengers must have run ahead because the general was waiting for them at the entrance. He was dressed in full military uniform and despite his age he stood tall and erect, a soldier from his toes to his fingertips.

"Please wait here, Sulpicius," he said gravely. "Consul, come inside and bring my nephew. Aurelia would never forgive me if anything happened to him."

They crossed an extravagant courtyard twinkling with gold and silver mosaics and entered an elegant sitting room.

"Now, Sulla," the general said, wearily sinking into a chair, "what is the cause of this disturbance?"

"Sulpicius is a traitor! His mob trapped me in the Temple of Castor and Pollux. For that he must surely be punished. I am the Consul, after all."

"And yet, from what you have said, Senator Sulpicius appears to have more support than you."

"Only because he caught me off guard."

"Something a Consul should never be."

Sulla scowled. "General, I came to you because I know you love Rome. The city will suffer if this dispute between me and the Senate is not resolved. Support me and I will deal with Sulpicius once and for all."

"You mean have him killed?" Marius shook his head. "That won't do. Can't you see you have lost the respect of Rome?"

"Then what should I do?" Sulla sounded uncertain for the first time.

"My advice is to leave the city. Go and defeat the rebels who've been raiding our farms in the south. If you succeed, as I did against the Germanic barbarians, then the people will love you once more."

"You're telling me to quit Rome?" Sulla was flabbergasted.

"Advising."

"Advice from Marius is like an order from anyone else."

The old general shrugged. "You came to me."

Sulla was silent for a long moment. "You leave me little choice," he said at last, and he left without another word.

"Sir, I can't believe you convinced him to go," Gaius said admiringly. "I thought there would be war."

"I've humiliated one of Rome's proudest Consuls," Marius replied. "One day he will want revenge and then, unfortunately, I fear there will be."

12

DESPITE General Marius's grim warning, Rome soon returned to normal. With Sulla gone there were no more riots and instead the markets were full and the bathhouses packed. Although Gaius was relieved, the days were often dull and when he returned home from lessons the house was too quiet. Quintus was gone and his mother was often out and when she was home she was irritable, fretting over her dwindling savings and the cost of replacing Zoe. Despite Corax having reported the slave's flight to each of the city's sixteen gates, she had not yet been caught. It made Aurelia furious. *But at least,* Gaius thought to himself, *she hasn't yet discovered my charm is missing.* Each morning he begged the gods to keep it from her for one more day.

"What are you doing after lessons?" Alexander asked one morning. It was the first time they had bumped into each other since their visit to the bathhouse.

"Nothing," said Gaius, thinking of the empty afternoon ahead.

"Then come and see the Circus Maximus with me."

They spent hours touring the huge chariot racing track, with Alexander excitedly pointing out the accuracy of the stone buttressing, the curve of the arches and all sorts of other things that Gaius would never have noticed. From then onwards they spent most afternoons together, either wandering around Rome or in Alexander's apartment, where there was always a pot of something warm on the stove.

One afternoon, towards the end of Januarius, Gaius climbed the stairs to Alexander's top-floor flat. Ignoring the unpleasant whiff of boiling cabbage and too many dogs from the apartment below, he knocked on the door.

"Come in," shouted Alexander. "Help yourself to apple and cinnamon tea."

The flat was tiny – just one room divided by a curtain. On one side was a neat and tidy kitchen area, two wooden beds, and a table and bench. On the other was Alexander's father's surgery. This was lined with shelves and smelt of an aromatic mixture of herbs and spices.

"Where's your father?" asked Gaius once he'd poured a cup of tea and joined Alexander in the surgery.

"Today's been so quiet he decided to go to the market and get some supplies. He's asked me to put these in alphabetical order while he's out." Alexander pointed at an array of clay pots and glass jars. "Mother sent them on a cart from Ostia."

"I'll help," said Gaius. He picked up a bottle of rust-coloured liquid and read out loud: "Gladiator blood! What's that for?"

Alexander sighed as he put the jars in order on the

82

shelf. "Father tries to persuade his patients to let him use cures that will actually work, but Romans love these traditional medicines. The harder they are to come by, the more they prize them. That one's expensive, but not as much as this."

He held out a pot.

"What's in it?" asked Gaius.

"Fat, cut from the stomach of a dying gladiator. People believe it's good for colds."

Gaius wrinkled his nose at the foul-smelling creamy yellow sludge. "It's disgusting!"

"Believe me, other doctors have much worse stuff ... things Father wouldn't dream of stocking."

"Like what?"

"Do you know the most expensive medicine in Rome? The crushed brains of a baby."

Gaius grimaced. "How would a doctor get that?"

"Women leave unwanted newborns on the hills outside Rome. The cold night air kills them and the doctors come at dawn. Father says they crack their little heads like eggs, but he won't do it. If a patient wants that sort of medicine he sends them elsewhere."

Just then Georgio Theopolis returned home with a basket of mint, thyme and several bulbs of fennel. He was a stooped man with a long bushy beard and a grey ponytail.

"That's good, Alexander. Well done," he said surveying the neatly arranged jars. "And it's lucky I went to market today – it won't be open tomorrow or the day after that."

"Why?" asked his son.

The doctor rolled his eyes. "More bad news. The Senate has decided that Sulla can no longer lead Roman soldiers. They're taking away his command and it's bound to lead to trouble."

"Why have they done it?" asked Gaius.

"If Sulla defeats the southern rebels he will be popular enough to return as Consul and they don't want him back. So they've asked General Marius to take his place. Can you believe it? He could be Consul within the month."

Immediately Gaius thought of the vestal's riddle; he must tell his mother.

"I need to get home. Alexander, I'll see you tomorrow."

Without waiting for a reply he ran down the stairs of the shabby tenement block, out into the crowded lane and abruptly stopped. Blocking the doorway to his courtyard was a potted cypress tree; someone had died.

With a knot in the pit of his stomach he squeezed around the prickly cypress and found his mother in the dining room, her head in her hands.

"Is it Father?" he asked breathlessly.

Aurelia looked up. Mascara was streaked down her cheeks and her eyes were red and puffy.

"No. It's not Father."

He was bewildered. "Then who?"

"Quintus."

Gaius felt his knees almost buckle beneath him. It

was less than a month since he'd waved his brother off. "How?" he gasped.

"They were attacked by bandits on the road from Asculum to Ancona. Every one of them was killed – one hundred in all." Aurelia began frantically pacing the room. "The messenger said nobody has been ambushed on that road for years. I can't bear it. My first-born son lying there covered in flies ... not even decently buried."

She began to sob.

"I'm so sorry," said Gaius miserably. "What can I do? Shall I write to Father and let him know?"

Aurelia wiped her tears away with her stola. "I've already sent the messenger on to him. But there is one thing you can do. Quintus's charm belonged to your father and his father before that and I was keeping it for Quintus's son, but now you are my eldest boy so you and your heirs must have it." She opened the altar, picked up the square of linen and tipped out the round golden charm. "Give me yours. It's what the goddess expects."

It had happened. The moment Gaius dreaded.

Aurelia held out her hand.

"I don't want to swap," he said, desperately hoping to change her mind. "My charm belonged to General Marius."

"Don't be silly, Gaius. Not at a time like this."

"Why don't we wait until Father gets home?"

"That could be years. We mustn't wait. It's the sort of thing that could bring that curse back. Give it to me now."

"I can't," he admitted at last. "It's not here."

"What do you mean?"

Gaius could hardly get out the words. "I've lost it."

"When?"

"Two weeks ago."

His mother stared at him. "Two weeks! That's when Quintus was killed." She sank to the couch. "Do you realize what this means? You are responsible. You are an unlucky son and now the Julii will never recover their glory."

"Don't say that," begged Gaius. "I promise one day I'll make you proud."

"Leave me alone," answered Aurelia coldly. "You are no son of mine."

13

THAT night Gaius couldn't sleep. He tossed and turned until at last his mind was made up. In the morning he would tell his mother everything ... about Marta and Tribune Rufus Agrippa and Fulvia Pollo. Perhaps then she would understand and forgive him.

He pulled himself out of bed just after dawn, wrapped a scratchy woollen blanket around his shoulders and crept into the courtyard.

Flora was sitting on a bench grinding wheat between two stones. "If you're looking for your mother, master, she's gone."

"Where?"

"To Ancona to make sure Quintus is properly buried."

Gaius was stunned. "When will she be back?"

"She'll be away at least a month."

"Did she leave me a note?"

The cook slave frowned. "She left nothing, master. Not even a sestertii to run the house."

For the next few weeks all Gaius could do was keep to his usual routine. He rose at dawn and walked to Gnipo's apartment for his lessons in Latin, Greek, poetry and law and after lunch he visited Alexander or went to the baths.

"When is Mistress Aurelia returning?" Gnipo asked one morning. "She's been gone more than a month now. I'm surprised she would leave you alone for so long."

"She'll be back soon," said Gaius, not wanting to discuss Quintus or the row over his charm, even with someone as kindly as Gnipo.

"Well, I don't like the thought of you being home on your own," continued the tutor. "Not at a time like this."

"At a time like what?" asked Gaius.

"Rumours are swirling round the Forum about Sulla. He's said to be camping just north of the Rubicon River with six legions and he's showing no sign of telling his men to lay down their arms."

"What does that mean?"

"Under Roman law, a general cannot come south of the Rubicon River unless he leaves behind his men and weapons. It's to stop them from seizing power. If Sulla does come south, it will be a declaration of war."

"And revenge against Marius," said Gaius, thinking back to that night in the general's study. "My uncle once told me that he thought something like this might happen."

"Well if it does, I don't want you to be alone. Is there anywhere you could go?"

Gaius shook his head. "Don't worry about me," he said. "I'm not by myself. There's Flora and the other slaves."

"Slaves have a habit of disappearing at the first sign of

trouble. Is there nobody else you can stay with?"

"No, but Mother should be home by the end of the week."

"Well let's hope she is. It wouldn't be right to leave you any longer than that."

That night, to wile away the lonely evening, Gaius curled up next to the brazier in the dining room and read. He was soon absorbed in *The Odyssey*, a Greek tale of one-eyed giants, evil enchantresses and sirens. But when he reached for the fifth scroll the coals had turned to ash and the temperature was falling fast. He got to his feet and opened the shutter an inch. It was well past midnight and the moon was high in the sky.

Yawning, he picked up the oil lantern and the fifth scroll and headed off to his room. He pulled up his blankets intending to read only one last chapter but he read on and on, oblivious to the time. Suddenly there was a tremendous thud and shriek from next door. Gaius leapt from his bed and opened the window. In the distance was an orange glow. For a moment he mistook it for dawn but then remembered he was looking west, not east. It must be a fire! A missile whizzed through the air and he realized what had happened. Sulla had crossed the Rubicon and Rome was under attack!

Hastily he pulled on his tunic, leggings and cloak and ran to the kitchen.

"Flora! Wake up!"

There was no response. Her camp bed was empty and so was the tiny cellar beyond the kitchen where the other slaves slept in bunks. They had all fled! Even Canis the dog was gone.

Gaius ran into the street and saw to his horror smoke billowing from the neighbouring apartment block. Alexander's building was on fire.

Without thinking he dashed in, taking the steep stone steps three at a time. From every floor people poured out of their cramped apartments, clutching crying children or their few possessions. Gaius pushed past them. He had to make sure Alexander and his father were safe.

"Come down!" shouted a man. "It's dangerous. The fire is worse upstairs."

But Gaius didn't listen. At last he reached Alexander's flat. Black smoke filled the corridor, burning the back of his throat as he hammered on the door. "Alexander! Mr Theopolis! Are you in there?"

No response. There was a bucket of water on the landing. Quickly he tore a strip of linen from his cloak, dunked it in the water, tied it over his mouth and nose, and then flung himself against the door.

"Alexander?" he cried again, as the flimsy lock gave way.

For a moment he couldn't see a thing and then, through the choking smoke, he saw Alexander on the ground. Gaius grabbed his arm. "Get up!" he screamed. "We have to get out of here!"

Choking, Alexander stumbled to his feet. "I can't leave him," he said thickly, pointing to where his father lay huddled in the corner.

"I'll get him." Gaius pushed Alexander towards the door just as a ceiling beam crashed down, sending thousands of cinders flying.

"What are you doing!" shouted a bearded man from the doorway. "The whole building's about to collapse! Get out."

"There's a man in here," yelled Gaius.

"You two go. I'll see what I can do. Hurry!"

Gaius dragged Alexander down the scorching steps. They seemed to go on and on but at last they reached the street, where a crowd of people were huddled together staring in horror at their burning homes.

"It's Sulla!" exclaimed a woman as Gaius sat Alexander down. "And I've heard General Marius is refusing to surrender! The whole city will be destroyed!"

"My father!" gasped Alexander between coughs.

"Wait here and I'll see if he's safe," said Gaius.

He started back towards the tenement block but suddenly the bearded man came tearing out. "Get back! It's going!"

He grabbed Gaius's hand, dragging him so hard he could hardly keep up. There was a terrifying rumble and then a blast knocked Gaius to the ground. He lay there for a moment, his ears ringing. He was covered in grit and dirt. Groggily he turned and looked behind him.

Where the apartment block had once stood was a heap of smouldering rubble.

Slowly Gaius pulled himself up, rubbing the dirt from his eyes. The bearded man was lying next to him, his hair matted with grey dust.

"Did you find Alexander's father?"

He nodded grimly. "Too late. The smoke got him. You will have to tell the boy."

14

"I MUST stay with Father."

Alexander stared at the remains of his home. All the neighbours had fled, scared off by the crashes and thuds of distant street battles, and the lane was eerily empty.

"You can't," said Gaius wearily. "Sulla's men will be here soon. You'll be killed."

"I can't leave him!"

"But what about your mother? You must survive for her."

Alexander shivered in his thin nightgown and wiped away a tear. "She'll never find me in this mayhem."

"Yes she will. Now come on. You need to get warm. We can hide in my house until the worst is over."

Gaius pulled Alexander to his feet and together they walked down the lane but when they entered the courtyard it was almost unrecognizable. The rooms on the left side of the atrium were covered with a shower of rubble and the floor was hidden by a thick layer of dust.

"Go to the kitchen. There might still be a fire in there," said Gaius grimly. "I'll see if I can find you some clothes."

Leaving a trail of footprints in the powdery dirt, he went into his bedroom. A part of the ceiling had fallen in, but he managed to get to his chest and pull out a cloak, a tunic, leggings and a pair of sandals. They were covered in dust but they would do.

He went back to the kitchen to find Alexander sitting on Flora's camp bed, his teeth chattering. The fire had burnt out and the room was dark apart from a square of moonlight coming through a small window.

"Put these on. I'll find you something to drink," said Gaius.

But as he was pouring a teaspoon of honey into a cup he heard voices.

"We're going to miss all the good stuff," a man was complaining. "By dawn, I'm telling you, everything will be gone."

Signalling for Alexander to stay quiet, Gaius crept to the window and peered cautiously over the ledge. Two soldiers in scarlet cloaks and leather breastplates were standing in the courtyard.

"Look, Clodius," moaned a tall redheaded one, "I want my fair share of loot too, but you heard General Sulla. Every member of the Marian, Julii and Sulpician families must be rounded up first."

"But no one's here," protested the other soldier. "Look at the state of the place. I say we take a look at that shop down the alley."

Please make them go, Gaius silently prayed to the gods – but just then the redheaded man replied, "No. Look! There are footprints in the dust. Someone is here!"

15

THE two centurions were almost at the kitchen door and at any moment the boys would be discovered. Gaius frantically looked around but there was nowhere for them to hide.

"Let's look in here," said one of the soldiers.

Gaius and Alexander were watching in horror as the latch lifted when suddenly someone called out, "Masters, I saw the Julii flee."

Gaius held his breath, praying that he and Alexander would be spared … and then the latch dropped. He couldn't believe his luck. Who had saved them?

When he was certain Sulla's soldiers had left the courtyard he opened the kitchen door just a little. Standing in the atrium was a skinny girl in a grey shift dress. She had very short dark hair, and a turned-up nose. It was Zoe, the runaway slave.

She raised a slender arm, as if asking for a truce, and walked cautiously towards him.

"What are you doing here?" Gaius asked.

"You saved me, master. It's my turn to repay the debt."

He stared at her in disbelief. "Then why did you betray me to Rufus Agrippa?"

Zoe looked bewildered. "Master, I don't know what you're talking about."

She's lying, thought Gaius. Apart from his mother and Flora, she was the only other person who knew of his curse.

"If you didn't tell him about me, why did you run away?" he asked roughly.

"Because I hated it here. I wanted my freedom."

"Then you should have earned it through loyal service like every other slave."

"You mean like Flora?" asked Zoe. "She's worked for you for twenty years and your mother still refused to let her go. In the end she was so unhappy that when a tribune came around offering to pay good money for information about you she took his sestertii. She told me it was so that when the time was right, she could afford to go. In fact I guess she's already gone. War is the perfect time to disappear."

A tribune wanting information about me, thought Gaius. *Flora was the traitor! Zoe wasn't to blame!*

"Why did you come back today?" he asked more gently.

"I found it impossible to escape the city – there are guards at every gate checking for runaways. So I hung around the busiest markets living off scraps, praying I wouldn't be noticed in the crowds. Then I overheard a couple of Sulla's men discussing the Julii and I knew you were in danger."

A sudden explosion in the distance shook the building, throwing up clouds of dust.

"We should leave," said Alexander, who had been listening to them in silence. "We're not safe here."

"He's right, master. Sulla's men are cutting his enemies' throats in the Forum. There are already piles of bodies."

"If there's nowhere safe in Rome," said Gaius, "we must try to leave the city."

"It'll be difficult," said Zoe. "There are soldiers everywhere – only the rats may roam as they please."

Rats! Gaius had an idea. "Then we'll copy them."

"How?" asked Alexander.

"We're not far from the bathhouse. Remember Petronius said the sewer tunnel was wide enough for a man. That's the way out of the city. Come on."

They reached the courtyard entrance and Zoe bowed her head. "Good luck, master. I wish you well."

"You're coming with us," said Gaius. "It's better if we stick together."

Although the Subura lanes were deserted there was always the chance of being spotted by one of Sulla's men so they made their way carefully. At every corner they stopped to check there were no soldiers about and they were relieved when at last the narrow lanes broadened into a grand square.

"The baths – over there," whispered Gaius.

There were always people milling around the marble bathhouse entrance but today the place was forsaken. They dashed across the cobbled stones, climbed the steps and then cautiously Gaius pushed open the front door.

"Is there anyone inside?" whispered Alexander.

"I don't think so," answered Gaius but just then a voice called, "Who's there?"

Gaius noticed a crumpled soldier with snow-white hair sitting propped up against the far wall. He was relieved; this old man couldn't do them any harm. But then the soldier turned and he saw his face. It was General Marius. Immediately he was at his uncle's side. "Sir, it's me – your nephew."

"Thank the gods," mumbled Marius. "You must help me. I wasn't prepared for Sulla's attack and I didn't have enough men. But there are loyal legions outside the city. I've sent a message to them and now all I need is to get back to my men in the Forum. They must think I've deserted them."

"Master, every soldier in the Forum was killed," said Zoe, crouching next to Gaius.

The general groaned as he struggled to his feet. Gaius saw he had a gash in his left calf. "You're hurt!"

Marius waved him away. "It doesn't matter."

"It does." Gaius quickly tore a strip of linen from his cloak. "Let me bandage it."

General Marius slumped to the ground but as soon as the wound was dressed he tried to heave himself up once more.

"Your men are dead, sir. You must stay here," Gaius said.

"I must die with my men."

"The prophesy says that you will serve seven terms as Consul."

"Then the augurs made a mistake," said Marius wearily.

"And what about Sulla?"

"Others will defeat him."

"But who? No one can lead men like you."

The old man shrugged. "I can't if I'm stuck in Rome."

"You're not," said Gaius excitedly. "We can get you out of the city."

16

"WAIT here and I'll make sure there's no one about," said Gaius.

Cautiously he scouted the nearest changing rooms, pool and gym but there was not a slave or a patron to be seen.

"There's no one here," he reported. "Let's go."

Gaius led the small party from the grand entrance hall into the dingy corridor where Petronius had shown them the door to the sewer.

"There it is." He pointed at a small doorway. "Alexander, stay here with General Marius. Zoe, come with me. We need torches."

They found two oil lanterns in a storeroom and lit them.

"I'll go down first to check it's all right," said Gaius. "Come when I give you the all clear."

He opened the sewer doorway and was instantly overwhelmed by a sulphurous stench so strong he almost gagged. *Stop it. You've got to do this*, he told himself as he edged down the steep steps. He held up the lantern and shuddered as a horde of tiny furry animals scampered off into the shadows. Rats! The smell grew worse. *Just breathe and you'll get used to it*, he told himself, though the thought revolted him.

He climbed down further. It was dark and cold but gradually his eyes adjusted to the gloom and he realized he was standing in a large stone tunnel. The curved ceiling was marked with patches of moss and dripped in places. Below moved a slow stinking stream of water with a narrow walkway down one side. At least they wouldn't have to wade through whatever vile things were in that stream.

"Come down!" he called over his shoulder.

Moments later Marius, Alexander and Zoe joined him on the narrow footpath.

"Zoe, you go ahead with one light," said Gaius, his voice echoing against the stone walls, "and Alexander, bring up the rear with the other. I'll help the general."

Gaius put an arm around Marius but the narrowness of the walkway meant they made slow progress in the lonely, dank tunnel. Their lights cast strange shadows and from time to time they heard the creepy pitter-patter of tiny feet and the splash of rats leaping into the water. Gaius was beginning to feel that they were never going to get out of this underground tomb when at last Zoe hissed, "I see a light!"

He peered into the distance. She was right. There, far off, was a tiny white spot. It must be the dawn sun.

"We've almost done it," he said excitedly.

They plodded on and the pinprick of light grew and

grew until they were only yards from the entrance to the tunnel. Golden sunlight streamed in through a tangled knot of ivy and the air was fresher.

"Wait here," whispered Gaius. "I'll see if there's anyone out there."

He tiptoed to the mouth of the tunnel and pushed the vines aside. At the entrance was a waterfall where the sewage poured over the rocks into a broad meandering river. On one side was a wide sandy cove and on the other, several hundred yards away, an arched bridge – the main route into Rome from the coast. Gaius could see soldiers patrolling on the bridge but he thought that if they went the other way they would soon be out of sight of them.

He ran back to tell the others. "Follow me. As long as we're careful, no one will see us."

General Marius smiled. "Nephew, the gods have blessed you."

Gaius blushed with pleasure and squeezed his empty charm pouch. Perhaps Venus wasn't so angry with him after all. Perhaps now the curse had been lifted.

17

GAIUS and Alexander stood at the edge of a wood, several miles from Rome. They had spent the morning walking along the banks of the River Tiber with Zoe and General Marius. Marius's wound was no longer bleeding and he seemed to gain strength as they got further and further from the defeated city. Now, for the first time, they were sufficiently far away to feel safe enough to rest.

"My army is camping just the other side of this forest," said Marius. "You can stay there as long as you like."

"That's kind, sir," said Gaius, "but it's time for me to find my mother."

He'd been thinking about her all morning.

"Do you know where she is?" asked the general.

"No. She left a month ago to bury Quintus."

Marius looked thoughtful. "I told her at the games that if there was ever any trouble she should go to Solonium."

"Where's that?" asked Gaius.

"It's my country estate – a day's walk away. If you want to try there, I'll see if I can spare a couple of centurions to accompany you."

"You can't do that, sir," said Gaius, "not when you have Sulla's legions to fight."

"And Gaius won't be alone," said Alexander. "I'll go too."

Gaius stared at him. "But you need to find your own mother."

"I have no idea where to look. I know she was on her way to Rome but she could have gone anywhere once she heard about the siege."

"Alexander, it's too dangerous. Sulla's not hunting your family but he is after mine."

"I'll take the risk. I want to ... to repay you for what you tried to do for my father. It's what he would have wanted."

"Thank you," said Gaius gratefully. "And once we've found my mother, we'll search for yours."

"And what about the slave?" asked the general. "Do you want to leave her here with me? With an army to feed there's always work in the kitchen."

Gaius caught Zoe's eye. She was too proud to say so, but he could tell it was the last thing she wanted.

"No," he said. "Zoe will come with us."

Not long after they reached the army camp, Marius handed Gaius a sealed scroll.

"Here is a message for my wife. She will make you welcome. My scouts report that Sulla's soldiers are east of here, so you should be safe. Follow the path until you reach the Via Flaminia, then head west. Once you've crossed the mountains you'll see the town of Nola on the coast. Solonium is just south of it. You should be there by sunset. Good luck."

* * *

By mid-morning Gaius, Alexander and Zoe were on their way with a satchel of rye bread, cheese and a carafe of goat's milk. They walked briskly along a muddy path, skirted ploughed fields and soggy marshes, and entered a cool dark forest. A hundred yards in they found a fast running stream where they scooped up handfuls of water. As they stood up to leave, Zoe took something from a leather pouch and kissed it.

What's that?" asked Gaius.

"A statue of Zeus, master. I was thanking him for the water."

Zeus is a Greek god, thought Gaius, realizing he knew nothing about Zoe.

"Where are you from?" he asked her as they picked up speed once more.

"Thrace, master. A few hundred miles north east of Athens."

"And how did you come to be a slave?"

"I was working in my family's olive grove with my brothers when some Romans crept up on us with nets."

"But Rome isn't at war with Thrace. Why would they capture you?"

"In my country Roman slave-traders catch anyone they can. Children are warned never to wander away from the village by themselves. That's why I was with my brothers – they don't usually pick on groups of people."

"And you hadn't attacked them? You were just unlucky?"

"No, master. We were just unlucky."

"And then what happened to you?"

Zoe frowned. "We were tied together with chains around our necks and put on a ship bound for Italy with many other slaves. We were crammed in so tightly we could hardly move and the sea was so rough, I was sick for days. But when we landed at the Port of Ostia things got much worse."

"What do you mean?"

"We were hosed down, shaved and locked up in cages right there on the quay and people came and poked at us as if we were animals. Different slave dealers bought us and I haven't seen my brothers since. But before we were separated, we made a pact – that somehow we would get home, or die trying."

As Zoe finished speaking the muddy path emerged from the dense copse. Ahead were several ploughed fields and the Via Flaminia. It was one of the oldest roads in Rome, an impressive dead-straight stone thoroughfare cut through the countryside. Wide enough for two carriages, it ran all the way from the capital to the coast.

As they crossed the last field Gaius saw that on the north side of the road, at intervals of around a hundred yards, there were several huge timber crosses. On one of them hung the body of a man. For a moment he was appalled. After listening to Zoe's terrible story it seemed cruel that she should see the brutal punishment inflicted on fleeing slaves. But he quickly decided it was better this way. She had to be realistic. He might be able to save her this time, but if she ran away again this would be her fate. The sooner she gave up on her dreams, the better.

They walked along the road in silence but when they reached the man on the cross, Zoe stopped. It was a gruesome sight. His feet were nailed to the timber pole, his arms were splayed and flies buzzed continually around his grossly swollen body.

"So this is a crucifixion," she said at last. "The poor man probably took days to die. It's so cruel. That's why I hate this country."

Gaius didn't know what to say. If the punishment for running away wasn't brutal, slaves would flee all the time.

"We must have slaves," he answered. "We need them."

"My village doesn't have any and we manage. Why can't Rome learn to manage too?"

Gaius paused ... she didn't understand ... Rome was different.

"Who would clean the streets, work in the baths, serve at tables, or look after the fields if there were no slaves?" he said at last. "Roman citizens can't do those things. It's beneath us."

"But not beneath me?"

He smiled. "Not beneath you, perhaps." But then he thought of everything that had happened and his smile faded. Rome couldn't let every slave go, but it didn't need this one. "Zoe, I promise you," he said solemnly, "that when we get home I'll find a way to give you your freedom. But until then you must stay with me. A runaway slave always gets found and this is what happens to them."

"Didn't your mother promise Flora her freedom when she was young?" asked Zoe. "Why should I believe you?"

"Because I *will* do it," said Gaius.

And he meant it.

18

LATE that afternoon, after a long tiring climb, they finally reached the mountain pass.

"That must be Solonium." Gaius pointed towards a glittering white villa close to the seashore south of Nola.

Alexander had been silent for most of the climb and Gaius knew that he was thinking of his father, but now he answered, "And there's its aqueduct." Alexander gazed at a sandy-coloured line of arches snaking down the valley. "It's bigger than I expected. The house must use gallons of water."

"Mother came to stay here once," said Gaius, hoping to distract his friend from the terrible fate that had befallen his father. "She couldn't believe the gardens and swimming pools. The estate has even got its own zoo and fish farm with eels, sea bass and red mullet so you can eat fresh fish whenever you want to. What would you say to salmon for supper?"

"I've never eaten it," admitted Alexander, smiling for the first time since they'd left Rome.

"Neither have I, but I wouldn't mind giving it a try."

They began to walk downhill. Alexander and Gaius led the way with Zoe following a few paces behind. By the time they crossed the plain and reached the edge of the estate the sun was low in the sky.

"Thank the gods we're here," said Gaius, as they approached a gate set in a high concrete wall decorated with a wrought-iron sculpture.

"There are no guards," said Alexander. "Should we just go in?"

"We don't have much choice."

They pushed open the heavy gates and hurried down a gravel drive that twisted steeply downhill past immaculate lawns, stunning mosaics, fountains and cages of exotic animals dozing in the last of the day's sun. But nowhere was there a slave to be seen.

"It's odd there's no one about," said Alexander. "You'd think a place like this would need hundreds of gardeners."

The absence of people was beginning to unnerve Gaius too. "That's just what I was thinking."

"And why are the animals so quiet?" said Zoe.

She's right, Gaius thought. *We haven't heard so much as a grunt. What's going on?* He crossed to the nearest cage, an ornate metal structure littered with straw. Two magnificent lions were flopped across the floor but as he got closer Gaius could see they weren't sleeping. They'd been killed by arrows in their soft bellies. He rushed to the next cage. A leopard with a diamond collar was lying in a pool of blood. *Why would anyone do this?* he thought frantically. *These animals cost a fortune.* Then he realized what it meant; Sulla's men had come calling. And for all he knew they were still here.

He waved his arms, signalling to Alexander and Zoe to get off the road.

"Sulla's men?" asked Alexander when he saw what was in the cage.

"I think so."

"Marius said they were east of Rome."

"He was wrong."

"His wife and children could be in trouble."

Gaius was thinking the same thing – and of his own mother. "I know," he said. "Stay here and I'll go to the house to find out."

"You shouldn't go alone."

"I must. There's less chance of being seen. Don't worry. I'll be as quick as I can."

Grateful for the long evening shadows he darted from one tree to the next, following the road down the steep valley until it turned sharply right and there, ahead of him, was the sprawling villa covered with purple and pink bougainvillea vines.

Cautiously he crept across the black and white chequered terrace and peeked into the grand atrium. Several statues lay smashed on the floor and the ornate marble pond in the centre was covered with a grisly carpet of limp, silver fish floating among the lilies.

Really frightened now, Gaius hurried past the gruesome pool and looked into the nearest room, a large library lined with shelves of scrolls. Two hideously wounded bodies – slaves – were lying next to a bronze candelabrum. Quickly he went on. There were bodies in every room among the slashed silks, smashed glass and precious vases. Not even the child slaves had been spared. Over and over again he prayed that this terrible fate had not befallen his mother and was relieved when he'd finished searching and found no sign of her. Thank the gods, she must have ignored Marius's advice.

"Did you find anyone?" asked Alexander when he returned to the leopard's cage.

"Sulla's men have murdered all the slaves and they must have done it recently – none of the bodies smells yet."

"Are the soldiers still around?"

"No."

"Then perhaps it would be safer to stay the night here. It's getting dark."

"We can't," said Gaius. "For one thing, the water has been poisoned, and for another there are too many valuable things lying around. I'm sure Sulla's men took some stuff but it won't be long before they are back for the rest." He didn't add the third reason – that after all he had seen, he couldn't bear to stay a moment longer.

"Where can we go at this time of night?" asked Alexander.

"I don't know," said Gaius. "Nowhere's safe."

"There is one place that could be," said Zoe. "I grew up in the mountains. No one will find us there."

* * *

Before leaving Solonium Gaius forced himself to go back to the house. He grabbed a few blankets and took some bread and salami from the kitchen.

They trudged off once more but this time they kept clear of the road and cut across country through hip-high grass, orchards and claggy ploughed fields. It was much more tiring than walking along the Via Flaminia and they were soon exhausted.

By the time they finally reached the foothills there was just a sliver of moonlight to see by.

"Which way now?" asked Gaius, leaning on a wooden fence. Ahead was a last field of goats and beyond that, steep rugged slopes.

Zoe gazed up at the lumpy mountains silhouetted against the night sky.

"The higher the better, master."

She surveyed the ridge carefully and then pointed at a summit, three peaks to the left. It was blunter than the rest, with a distinctive square top.

"Why that one?"

"Partly because it reminds me of home," she admitted. "My village was just below such an odd-shaped peak. But also because from there we'll have a better view of the valley. And, master, before we start climbing, there's one last thing we need – a goat."

Before Gaius had a chance to protest that surely they could do without milk for a few days, Zoe hopped over the fence into the field. Skilfully she separated a large white goat with stumpy horns and bloated udders from its frightened kid, pinning it in the corner of the meadow. Then she pulled the sash from her tunic and tied it around its neck. The goat wasn't happy and, as Zoe dragged it back across the meadow, it protested loudly, its pitiful bleats travelling far in the still night air.

"We can't take that thing," said Gaius. "If Sulla's men are around, it'll give us away."

"It's not Sulla's men we need to worry about," said Zoe. "These hills are full of wolves. The goat won't just give us milk; she's our warning system. If a wolf comes within thirty yards she'll make such a noise we won't be able to sleep through it. Now come on. We should get halfway up the mountain before we stop for the night."

Zoe led the way, with Alexander and Gaius taking turns to drag the obstinate goat. As the hill became steeper, Gaius half wished the slave would slow down but the tougher the slope the more effortlessly Zoe seemed to pick her way over boulders and craggy rocks.

At last they reached a narrow grassy ledge below a cliff.

"We'll stop here for the night," said Zoe, to Gaius and Alexander's relief.

As soon as they stopped moving, the three of them felt the cold but Zoe warned them that a fire would be easy to spot. So they tethered the goat to a large flat stone, ate all but a last hunk of bread and wrapped themselves in the blankets. The ground was rocky, damp and uncomfortable but Gaius was so tired that in no time he was asleep.

"Wake up!"

Gaius rolled onto his side. *It can't be morning already!* he thought.

"Wake up, I said!"

He opened his eyes. The sky was grey and misty. Alexander was crouching beside him and he could hear the goat's rasping bleats.

"What is it?" he asked groggily. "Wolves?"

"I'm not sure. Zoe told me to quieten this thing but I don't know how."

Gaius threw Alexander the last crust of bread. "Give her that." And then he went over to Zoe who was standing some distance away, listening intently.

"What is it?"

"Not wolves. There are no howls and anyway they prefer the night."

"Then what?"

"I heard a twig snap above us and a pebble fall below."

"So?"

"I think it's Sulla's men ... and I think we're surrounded."

19

FROM out of the mist stepped a wiry tanned man with a shaved head and one gold earring. He was dressed in a loincloth and was holding a spear.

Gaius spun around but on the far side of the ledge was another man armed with a dagger.

"Who are you?" asked the first man in heavily accented Latin.

"We're slaves," said Zoe quickly.

The man lowered his weapon an inch.

They must be runaways, Gaius realized, *hiding up in the hills.*

"Where are you from?"

"Rome." Zoe spat on the ground. "We worked for the Julii, the gods curse them. One of those stuck-up Roman families – not much money but as blue-blooded as they come. General Marius is a relative and don't they let you know it."

The man eyed her curiously. "You don't sound like you were born here."

"I'm from Thrace. I've only been a slave for two months and that was enough."

"And the boys?"

Gaius held his breath. Would Zoe turn on them and give them away? But instead she pointed at Alexander. "He's Greek and he's called Alexander. He's been here since he was a baby." She paused. "And he's Italian... Luca is his name... He was caught a few years ago in the Social Wars."

Gaius did his best to hide his relief. Zoe had done well. There were hundreds of Greek slaves in Rome and Italians sounded exactly the same as Romans.

The man with the spear turned to him. "How long have you worked for the Julii family?"

"Many years."

"You don't sound like a slave."

"He came from one of those rich Italian families," explained Zoe hurriedly. "They even had him educated. He can read and write. He worked for the Julii as a scribe."

Gaius was impressed; Zoe was doing well.

"And what did you do for these Julii Romans?" the man asked Alexander.

"I worked like a skivvy in their kitchen. We ran away together just a few days ago during the battle for Rome and decided to head for the mountains."

The man smiled. "You've come to the right place. I'm Pedro. I'm from Hispania and Axel here is from Germania. We escaped three months ago from one of the farms down in the valley. We're not alone; there are around a hundred of us hiding out up here because the Romans are too lazy to search the mountains. We're planning to stay until it's safe to cross the Alps and make our way home."

"With the masters tied up with their war, why not go now?" asked Gaius, thinking it was about time he opened his mouth.

"The passes in the Alps are blocked with snow," said Pedro. "And anyway our scouts say it won't be long before General Sulla is victorious and things settle down again. His men reached Nola yesterday morning and they're rounding up the aristocrats."

Was that what happened to my mother and General Marius's family? thought Gaius. *And if so, where are they now?*

Pedro glanced at Axel and then said, "Do you want to join us? We have enough supplies."

The last thing Gaius wanted was to join a camp of treacherous slaves but Zoe answered for them all. "Yes we do," she said quickly. "Thank you. We'll pack up our camp."

Soon they were following Pedro and Axel up the mountain, the German with the goat slung around his shoulders and the Spaniard carting a large sack of turnips.

"Are you sure this is a good idea?" Gaius whispered to Zoe as they fell a little behind.

"I don't think we had any choice. If we hadn't joined them they'd have been suspicious and who knows what they might have done."

"What if they discover who we really are?"

"We'll have to pray they don't," she answered, kissing her tiny statue of Zeus.

Gaius wished he had Marius's charm but it was stuck in Rome with that witch, Fulvia Pollo.

"Almost there," shouted Pedro when, after another steep climb, they reached a cliff. He whistled and a man appeared fifteen feet overhead.

"These friends are going to join us."

Pedro led them along the side of the cliff until they reached a narrow opening. One after another they squeezed though the gap and found themselves in a ravine overgrown with ivy.

They scrambled over several large boulders to the end of the gully. "Use the vines to climb," Pedro told them, grabbing a twisted stalk and nimbly heaving himself up.

"You next, Luca," he shouted.

Gaius took hold of a thick stem and clambered up the crag. His arms ached and he made slow progress but at last he reached the top. He gasped. Below him was a circle of white canvas tents in a large grassy bowl with a couple of toddlers playing happily in the mud.

Pedro smiled. "Everyone is always surprised. It's an extinct volcano and those tents are stolen from an army camp. It's wonderful, isn't it?"

"Incredible," said Gaius.

"I'm glad you like it. Welcome to your new home."

ONE YEAR LATER

MAY, 87 BC

20

"LUCA, wake up! You're on scout duty."

Gaius pulled himself out of bed, grabbed his sandals and climbed to the top of the ridge – the entrance to the crater. Spread out beneath him was a stunning view of the entire west side of the mountain and beyond that the plain, divided into a patchwork of fields, and the sea.

He settled down, cross-legged on a smooth grey rock warmed by the early morning sun. The air was so clear he could see rippling waves and a tiny fishing boat bobbing around. Until noon it was up to him to ensure that nobody got near the camp so he carefully surveyed the woods and the trees on the slopes. If he saw anything suspicious he had to whistle and the runaways would come to his aid.

One morning, around a month after Gaius, Alexander and Zoe arrived at the camp, Axel was on guard and sounded the alarm. Gaius was amazed to see how quickly the men dropped whatever they were doing, grabbed a weapon and ran to the entrance, while the women and children climbed down vines on the far side of the crater and hid in caves until the danger had passed. Fortunately that time it had been just a couple of wild boars, snuffling and digging in the ground – but one day it could be Romans.

"You're up early," said Gaius, as Alexander climbed up onto the rocks to join him.

"I wanted to talk. Do you know how long we've been here?"

Gaius was surprised. "No. But a long time."

"I think it must be more than a year. The vegetables we're eating now are turnips, just like when we first came."

Each day the runaways caught what game they could find on the mountain – rabbits, squirrels, even the odd piglet – and from time to time a party would venture down to the plains to steal fruit and vegetables from the local farms. Pedro and Axel had been returning from just such a trip when they'd stumbled across Gaius, Alexander and Zoe on the ledge.

"You're right," said Gaius. Then he lowered his voice. "I wonder how much longer we should stay."

When they'd joined the camp, Gaius had assumed they would run away at the first opportunity, but Zoe had persuaded him not to. They were safer here, she'd argued. Until Sulla was defeated, Rome was too dangerous and where else could they go? And so they had remained, month after month, scouting the mountains and hunting, fetching water from the nearest stream and cutting logs. Pedro had a never-ending list of chores. He constantly reminded the runaways that the camp was not their permanent home and when it was time to move on, they must be ready. For the long trek north each of them would need a blanket, spare shoes, clothes, weapons and as much dried fruit as they could carry. There was too much to be done to waste a single hour.

A benefit of the constant activity was that Gaius, Alexander and Zoe had little time to dwell on the lives they'd left behind. On the rare occasions when the scouts picked up news from the outside world it was never good. Marius had attacked Sulla but had been easily defeated. He had fled to Carthage in North Africa, leaving Sulla the undisputed dictator of Rome.

Pedro climbed on to the ridge. "Morning boys. I'm going to take a look around."

He grabbed two thick vine stems and shimmied down into the ravine.

Alexander waited until Pedro was at the bottom of the gorge before saying to Gaius, "Do you think he really wants to leave? He always finds a reason to put it off."

Gaius thought for a moment. Last summer when the Alps were passable, it had been too dangerous to go. Sulla's centurions were everywhere looking for enemies and a band of runaway slaves would easily have been caught. But surely this summer they must leave, and yet it was true that Pedro always found some reason or other to delay.

"I'm not sure. He's very cautious. Perhaps he's scared to risk it after all this time."

"I suppose it suits us," said Alexander. "But we must be ready to get away if Pedro ever gives the order. We can't go north with them."

"Luca," Pedro shouted from the ravine below. "I'm coming up! And I've got someone with me."

He climbed up and was soon followed by a powerfully built man with black curly hair and gold earrings.

"Get a move on!" the stranger shouted down into the canyon, "I haven't got all day." *He has the same accent as Zoe*, thought Gaius as the man tugged on a rope tied around his waist.

"Are you sure she can't escape?" asked Pedro.

"Certain. I've checked the rope a hundred times."

"A Roman aristocrat," Pedro explained to Gaius and Alexander. "We can barter her for our freedom if we get caught heading north."

A Roman! thought Gaius.

From below came a whiney, tearful voice. "I can't do it. I'm not strong enough."

"Perhaps you should help her," Pedro suggested to the stranger. "You can see the girl's never done an honest day's work in her life. She might not be able to manage."

"It's about time she learned." The stranger sat down on a rock to sun himself, occasionally pulling sharply on the rope that dangled down into the ravine. "Have you heard that General Marius has landed back in Italy?"

Gaius pricked up his ears. This was the first good news they'd had in ages.

"I knew he was on his way from Africa," said Pedro cautiously.

"Not just on his way. He's set up camp in the port of Ostia with over five thousand men. That'll give Sulla something to think about. I tell you, those Romans will soon be at war with each other again. It's the perfect time for us to get away."

Just then a girl in a torn grubby blue toga clambered over the edge of the ridge. Her blond hair was dishevelled, she was flushed and sweaty, and a cord was tied so tightly round her foot that her toes were purple.

"You'll pay for this!" she said defiantly as she flopped to the ground panting heavily. Hot angry tears tumbled down her cheeks. "All of you will pay. I'll see to it." And then she stopped and stared at Gaius. "By Jupiter, what are you doing here, Gaius? Did one of your slaves kidnap you as well?"

Gaius flinched. This was awful, but Pedro turned on her. "He's not called Gaius. His name is Luca and he used to work in the household of the Julii family. Too much sun has confused you."

"It most certainly has not," said the girl indignantly. "I'm Atia Cinna, Marius's niece, and that is one of his nephews. I recall him very well. Gaius, tell this traitor that I'm not mistaken!"

With a sinking feeling Gaius remembered the irritating girl who'd accused him of being scared of blood that day at the games. Then she'd looked like a little madam with her fancy hairdo, jewels and silk gown and now here she was, smeared with dirt and covered in scratches. No wonder he hadn't recognized her. He must keep his wits about him. He had lived with Pedro and the runaways for more than a year. Surely they would believe him over a disorientated Roman captive.

"You are mistaken. I've never seen you before," said Gaius as calmly as he could. "I was a slave in Rome."

"With an accent like that! I think not," said Atia, smirking. "You were sitting on the other side of my uncle in the Forum in Rome. I'd know you anywhere."

"You're wrong," said Gaius, praying she would shut up.

"No I'm not." By now the girl, who was evidently used to getting her own way, was angry. "Spartacus, you remember. Gaius was at the games the day your brother was killed."

The stranger looked hard at Gaius. "By the gods, you're right. And it was his brother who killed him." He frowned and drew a dagger from its sheath. "Pedro, you have a spy in your midst."

21

GAIUS stared at the razor-sharp blade gleaming in the sunlight. His insides churned. *Is this what Quintus felt like when he was attacked?* He wondered if he would be brave or did bravery just mean showing no sign of the terror you felt?

"Kneel," commanded Spartacus, "and show me your neck, just as my brother had to show his to entertain you Romans!"

Gaius dropped to the ground. *Get it over with, he prayed. If this is the way the gods want me to die, then the sooner the better.*

He tilted his face towards the sun and braced himself but suddenly Pedro pointed at Alexander. "Luca might not be the only one. I found them together."

Spartacus threw Alexander to the ground next to Gaius. "Then he should be killed too." He turned to Atia. "And you can finally make yourself useful. Tell Pedro who this is."

"You misunderstand your role, Spartacus," the girl answered haughtily as she cleaned the worst of the sweat and mud from her face with the edge of her toga. "It's not for me to make myself useful to you. You are my slave.

You should be serving me."

Spartacus slapped her, leaving a stinging red mark on her cheek.

"How dare you?" Atia snapped, eyes blazing. "When I get home, I'll make sure that you are whipped until you beg for mercy and then I'll have you crucified as well. How could you turn on me? Didn't my family feed and water you?"

Spartacus ignored her. "Tell us if you know this boy," he growled, holding a rope to her throat. "Or you'll be killed with them."

Atia glanced in Alexander's direction. "I don't recognize him."

"Spartacus, you're not getting anywhere," said Pedro. "Let me try." He turned to Alexander. "Are you a spy?"

"Neither of us is," Alexander gasped. "We're not slaves, but that doesn't make us spies. Gaius's family is being hunted by Sulla and my father was killed in the war in Rome. That's why we ran away. We came up here because we thought it would be safer. If we were spies do you really think we would have stayed this long?"

Spartacus gave Alexander a sharp kick. "Don't believe him."

"He's telling the truth," begged Gaius. "He's not even Roman."

"If you're not Roman, what are you?" demanded Pedro.

"Greek. My father was a doctor in Ostia and then Rome."

"Then he's as good as Roman to me," said Spartacus dismissively. "Kneel next to Gaius and say your prayers to your gods."

"Wait," said Pedro. "There was a girl with them as well. We need to find out if she's a traitor too. Follow me ... all of you ... and we'll get to the bottom of this."

He led the way into the crater and told a young woman to go and find Zoe.

As the woman scuttled off towards the furthest tent, Gaius prayed that Zoe had somehow got wind of their discovery and escaped but she was soon dragged to join them.

"You're all traitors," said Pedro angrily. "Kill them, Spartacus. I've had enough."

"I can't." Spartacus dropped his dagger. "She's my sister."

22

ZOE and Spartacus held each other for a long time while Pedro looked as bewildered as Gaius felt.

"Is Kiros with you?" Zoe asked at last.

Her brother shook his head. "He was killed in a gladiator fight. I was there when it happened."

Tears rolled down Zoe's cheeks. "When I saw this mountain, it reminded me of the one at the top of our valley. I thought it was a sign that all three of us would get home one day."

"I thought so too," said Spartacus. "And it *was* a sign. It's brought us back together. You and I will get back to Thrace."

Pedro waved his hands impatiently. "We have other matters to deal with. Zoe will be spared but not the boys."

Zoe dropped to her knees. "Spartacus, if it wasn't for Gaius, I'd be dead. You can't allow this to happen. Please!"

Spartacus frowned. "He's a Roman, Pedro, and I loathe them all as much as any slave does, but Gaius saved my sister and I think he tried to save my brother too, at the games in Rome. For that, I would rather he wasn't killed."

"And what about the other one?" said Pedro.

"Alexander's done nothing wrong," Gaius protested.

"He's only hiding here until it's safe to look for his mother."

"It's true," said Zoe. "He shouldn't be punished."

Pedro turned to Spartacus. "Tie both boys up and I will work out what to do."

Gaius woke. His neck was stiff, his arms ached and it was so dark he could hardly see a thing. That morning he'd been tied to the central shaft of one of the canvas tents. Alexander was opposite him and Atia behind – out of sight but, unfortunately, not out of earshot.

All day long, as they'd waited to hear their fate, Atia grumbled and complained. She whined about the heat in the airless tent, how thirsty and hungry she was and the cheek of Spartacus kidnapping her when he was her slave. Gaius became so exasperated that he'd shouted at her that they were all in the same position and that moaning didn't make it any better. He soon regretted it, for his sharp words only made her worse and it was only when Spartacus came that evening to tell them what Pedro had decided that Atia finally quietened.

"He called a meeting of the runaways," Spartacus told them. "And they decided that since General Marius has returned to fight Sulla this is the perfect time for us to head home. The Romans will be at war and the snow in the mountain passes has melted. We pack tonight and will leave at dawn tomorrow. The only question was, what to do with you?"

"And what did they decide?"

"Some wanted you killed, others wanted to take you north with us. But in the end they decided the simplest thing was to leave you tied up in this tent. Unlike you Romans, we are not murderers. The gods may save you if they wish."

By the time Spartacus gave them the news, Gaius's mouth was already painfully dry and his stomach ached for food. Now he knew that it was going to get worse ... much, much worse. *It's the worst possible outcome*, he'd thought. *We'll die of thirst and it will take days.*

Now, in the dead of the night, he twisted around, trying to ease his wrists a little. Perhaps if he could get more comfortable he could fall back to sleep. Anything rather than ponder their dreadful fate.

"Are you awake?"

Someone prodded him. Zoe was crouching beside him.

"What are you doing here?" he asked.

"Everyone's leaving. We want to be on our way before dawn." She pulled a penknife from a small linen bag and started hacking away at the cords around his wrist. "But I couldn't leave you tied up like this. This way you have a chance."

The rope loosened and Gaius tugged his hands free.

"Good luck." Zoe stood up. "I need to catch the others up before I'm missed."

"Don't go," said Gaius. "They're bound to be caught

and then they'll be crucified or sent to a gladiator camp and made to fight to the death. Stay with us instead. The only way for you to get home is for a Roman citizen to free you, and I've promised to find a way to do that, just as soon as we get back to Rome."

"I can't leave Spartacus."

"Then persuade him to come too. I'll find a way to free him as well."

"I've already tried. But he's adamant – no Roman owns him so no Roman can give him his freedom."

"Then let him try his way, and you yours."

She was silent for a while, gazing at him with her wide brown eyes. Then she said slowly, "All right. But I'm leaving my brother for the hope of freedom. So I'm relying on you to keep your promise."

"I will," said Gaius. "I swear. Now come on. There's no time to lose."

He saw that he'd convinced her and quickly shook Alexander awake.

"What about Atia?" asked Zoe.

Atia! The thought of bringing her along made Gaius's heart sink but he knew they couldn't abandon her.

"I suppose it wouldn't be right to leave her behind."

"I thought you'd say that," said Zoe, picking up her penknife once more.

23

"WHICH way?" asked Alexander, sitting down to rest on a fallen tree trunk.

So far they had been lucky. It was a clear night and they'd been able to pick their way down the steep slopes in the silvery moonlight. At first their progress was slow but once they'd reached the pungent pine forests they'd picked up speed.

"I don't know," admitted Gaius.

When they'd left the camp they'd had no time to think about where they were running to. The slaves were gathering on the far side of the crater for their long trek north and would quickly discover their Roman prisoners were missing so Gaius and the others had focussed on getting as far away as possible. Each time a twig snapped or an animal scuttled past under the cover of darkness, they'd held their breath, terrified the slaves were after them. Even Atia realized that they couldn't risk resting. She moaned incessantly about how tired she was but never once suggested that they stop.

It was only now, when the sun had risen and they could see fields at the edge of the forest, that they felt able to catch their breath. Surely even if the runaways were tracking them, they wouldn't risk being caught out on the open plain. *But are we swapping one danger for another?* wondered Gaius. *Could Sulla still be searching for people connected to Marius after all this time?*

"I need food," said Atia, flopping to the ground. "Soon!"

"It might be better to wait," suggested Zoe. "It's not wise to steal food in daylight."

"Don't you dare address me in that impertinent manner!"

"Stop it, Atia!" said Gaius. "If it weren't for Zoe, we'd still be prisoners."

"I'm just saying I need food. And I want to get home."

"We all want you to get home," Gaius replied through gritted teeth. "Believe me, the sooner, the better."

"Likewise," said Atia. "And when I do, I'm going to tell Uncle Marius about the way you've treated me."

"Marius!" said Gaius. "Of course! He's just landed at Ostia. We'll head for the port. Then you can tell Marius anything you want. And if we go cross country, we might even find some fruit to pick along the way."

All day long they tramped through orchards and fields, keeping well away from the occasional farmhouse or village, until at last they could see the sea shimmering on the horizon and the outskirts of a walled town.

"Wait here," said Gaius when they reached a cobbled road. "I'll see if I can find a slave who can tell us the best way into the port."

"No, I'll go," said Zoe. "The moment you open your mouth they'll know you're noble born."

Gaius knew she was right. Over the past year he'd grown taller and lankier, his hair was long and tangled and he was used to the rough wool tunic of a slave, but he still spoke with the polished Latin of a Roman aristocrat.

As Zoe walked away, Gaius, Alexander and Atia crouched down in the corner of a field of billowing golden corn to avoid being seen from the road.

"You know that girl may never come back," said Atia, spitting out the stones of some cherries they had found along the way. "I don't trust her an inch."

"Don't be ridiculous," said Gaius. "Think of what she's done for us."

"I don't care. If the past few days have taught me anything it's that you can never trust a slave. Look at Spartacus. My family tried to teach him how to serve and be civil, and he repaid them by snatching me from my bed in the middle of the night!"

Gaius said nothing. There was no point talking to Atia; she was too spoilt and she would never, ever accept that Zoe was different.

At last Zoe opened the field gate and came looking for them, shielding her eyes from the bright sunlight.

"Here!" Gaius called, lifting his head above the corn ears. "Any news?"

She jogged over. "It took ages but I finally found a slave picking peaches in an orchard."

"What did he tell you?"

"Just as Spartacus said. Marius has landed at Ostia and his men have taken over the town, and they're so worried about spies that unless you can prove that you live in Ostia, it's impossible to get in."

"Rubbish," said Atia dismissively. "I know many of Uncle's men. With me there, it'll be easy."

"I hope you're right," said Gaius.

"Of course I am. You'll see."

They were just a hundred yards from Ostia's imposing stone walls. Ahead was a wooden gate flanked by two sentries, one of whom was pointing his spear straight at them.

"Stop there. Don't take another step," he ordered.

"Put that down, Tiro!" said Atia. "It's me!"

The soldier squinted. "Miss Atia?" He stepped cautiously forward. "They said you'd been abducted."

"I was – and one day Spartacus will pay for his insolence. Escort us to my uncle. He'll want to know that I am safe."

"Certainly, madam," said the astonished soldier and moments later, as all four of them were ushered through the creaking gate, Atia smugly whispered, "Told you so."

Inside the high stone walls they found themselves in a small provincial town with a main square, a temple, law courts, shops and a busy quay with hundreds of boats. There were soldiers everywhere. Quickly Tiro led the children down several narrow lanes until they reached a pretty piazza with a whitewashed villa. More soldiers were milling around outside its gates but Tiro spoke to the guards and they had no difficulty in gaining entry to its leafy courtyard, where several important-looking men were waiting on benches outside double doors.

"I'll leave you here, madam," said the soldier. "As soon as General Marius is free he will send for you, but it may be a while. He's very busy at the moment, as you can see. Can I ask a slave to fetch you drinks while you wait?"

"Yes. And you can take her away." Atia pointed disdainfully at Zoe. "She should be kept in the slave quarters."

"Atia! You can't just send Zoe away," protested Gaius. "Not after all she's done."

"What's wrong with you?" Atia rolled her eyes. "Are you suggesting we bring a slave with us to meet Marius? He would think we'd gone mad."

Gaius blushed. She was probably right... But after living with Zoe for a year she felt more like a friend and sending her off would be awkward and ungrateful. However, he was spared further embarrassment when Zoe said, "I don't mind. In fact I'd prefer it. At least I'll get some peace."

Atia sank down onto one of the marble benches and glared as Zoe and Tiro disappeared through a tiny door on the far side of the courtyard. "Peace? She'd better not have been talking about me! And Marius too busy! It's not as if I've just come back from a trip to the market."

"I'm sure he'll send for you as soon as he can," said Alexander gently.

They settled down and watched one man after another disappear through the double doors and emerge sometime later carrying a scroll or a map.

The sun had sunk below the red-tiled roof when the last one hurried off and a man in a scarlet uniform came out of the study. He had dark curly hair, a large straight nose and thin colourless lips, and he walked in an unusually upright manner, as if he had a stick stuck up his back. Gaius stiffened as he realized it was Rufus Agrippa, the tribune who'd bribed Flora.

"Good day, Atia. The general apologizes for keeping you waiting so long. You can see he has too many demands on his time."

"I'm sure he does," said Atia grudgingly. "Perhaps you would be kind enough to take us to him now."

"Who should I say is with you?"

"Gaius Julius Caesar and Alexander Theopolis."

"Gaius of the Julii clan?" Rufus Agrippa smiled. "I hardly recognize you. You're so much taller – and scruffier! How good to see you."

Gaius was surprised by the warmth of the greeting and even more surprised when Rufus Agrippa embraced him.

"I owe you a great deal," said the tribune. "Now come. The general will be so pleased to see you."

Moments later they entered a grand study filled with

scrolls, busts of famous Roman Consuls and luxurious silk cushions. Marius was hunched over a broad mahogany desk with his back to them.

"Wait here," said Rufus and he whispered in the old man's ear.

Marius got to his feet and turned, his arms outstretched. Although he looked weary and frail, he smiled brightly.

"Gaius!" he exclaimed. "I knew you'd survive. The gods have great plans for you, my boy. I feel it in my bones. Welcome to you too, Atia. And your friend. Why don't you all come and sit by the fire and tell me of your adventures. There's not a better tonic for a worn out old man. Make sure you don't miss a thing!"

24

GAIUS, Alexander and Atia sat on stools by the fire with Marius and Rufus Agrippa. It was late, for the general had meant what he'd said – he wanted to hear every detail of their adventures. Occasionally Gaius or Atia had gone too fast or skipped over something and each time Marius had insisted they retell that part of the story.

When the candles burnt low, slaves brought in a meal of chickpea salad, honey-glazed ham, stuffed dates and custard. The children were famished and tucked in, savouring the delicious food, but Marius still wanted to hear more. He shook his head with dismay at what had happened to his estate at Solonium and slapped his knees with delight when Gaius told him of their escape from the camp.

"I'll dispatch a few of my men to find that lot," he declared, sending Rufus Agrippa off with the order. "It won't be long before they're caught."

Silently Gaius hoped Marius was wrong. After all, Zoe's brother was one of the runaways. Atia had no such scruples.

"Uncle, Spartacus must be particularly harshly punished," she said. "He was so cruel to me."

"Of course he'll be punished."

"But more than the rest?"

"More than the rest," agreed the general.

Atia smiled. "Good. And now may I go to bed? I'm exhausted."

"So am I, sir," said Alexander, his eyelids drooping.

"Of course."

Marius clapped his hands and a young slave, who could not have been more than seven years old, appeared at the door. "Zenobia will find you rooms for the night. Gaius, would you mind staying a moment longer?"

"Certainly, sir," Gaius replied, intrigued.

Once Atia and Alexander had gone, Marius leaned forward conspiratorially. "The gods must love you for you to have survived all your adventures. Tomorrow I march on Rome and I want you to come. You will bring me good fortune and I'm going to need all the luck I can get."

"I'd be honoured, sir," said Gaius, who wanted nothing more than to get home.

"And I want the slave – Zoe – to come too. To meet up with her brother like that, she must also be blessed by her gods."

Again the general clapped his hands and Zenobia appeared once more.

"Where is the slave who came with my nephew?"

"In the outhouse with the kitchen slaves, sir."

"Wake her and bring her here."

Once Zenobia had left Gaius steeled himself to ask

the question that had been on his mind for months. "Sir, what about my parents? Do you know what's happened to them?"

"Your father is still in the east and I believe your mother is alive."

"Are you sure?" Gaius asked excitedly. It was what he had prayed for, day after day in the runaway's camp.

"About your father, yes, and about your mother, I think so."

"Is she in Rome?"

"That I cannot say. Everything in the city is very difficult and confused. Sulla is so brutal, each morning his men post a list in the Forum of those he wants killed and the people can do nothing about it. It has to stop."

Marius threw another log on the fire and stared thoughtfully at the flurry of embers. "When I was a boy, not much younger than you, I was walking along a quiet lane when I felt my charm – the charm you now wear – slip from my neck. I turned to pick it up and was amazed to find an eagle's nest with seven eggs caught in my cloak hem. For a moment I thought the nest had fallen from a tree but there were no trees around. So I carefully picked it up and carried it home, and that evening my parents consulted a priest. I imagine you know what he said."

"I do, sir," said Gaius.

"Then you are familiar with the prophesy. When I had served my sixth term as Consul and was asked to make way for another I did so willingly, thinking perhaps the gods had made a mistake. Serving six terms was miraculous enough; I could not expect another. But the gods were not wrong. I saved Rome once and I must do it again. It is my fate and you will help me."

"Me?" Gaius was astonished. "How, sir?"

"Somehow our fortunes are linked." Marius leaned closer, his eyes shining brightly. "Tell me, have the gods sent you a sign?"

Gaius frowned. The only sign he could think of was the curse and he didn't want to tell Marius about that.

"Think hard," said the general.

Then Gaius remembered his pouch slipping off in the Temple of Vesta. Could this be what the general meant?

"Once," he said slowly, "the charm I inherited from you also untied itself for no reason."

"And what happened?"

"The Chief Vestal, Fulvia Pollo, was there and when she saw it she consulted the sacred flames and then she told me, 'The Julii will rise when the last egg hatches.'"

"The seventh egg! I knew it!" exclaimed the general. "You and I are bound together through the charm! If you come with me to Rome, it comes too and with it comes good fortune."

Gaius's heart sank. "There's something you should know," he said, dreading the general's response. "I don't have the charm any more. Fulvia Pollo took it."

"Fulvia Pollo?" said Rufus Agrippa, who'd returned and was sitting quietly by the fire. He turned pale. "It's just possible ... wait a moment ... I can't believe it."

He went off and moments later returned with an elegant young woman. Her red curls were piled on top of her head, she wore a stylish green dress and gold bangles, and her skin was so pallid she must have spent her life indoors.

"Is this your charm?" She held out her open hand.

There, twinkling in the candlelight, was the gold charm with its distinctive profile of the Goddess Venus.

Gaius stared at the stranger. "How is this possible?"

"Let me introduce you to my sister, Calpurnia Cotta," said Rufus Agrippa.

Gaius was bewildered. "Calpurnia Cotta? The vestal?"

"The very same – the girl whose life you helped save."

Gaius stared at her. "How can I have saved you? I've never met you."

"But you have met Marta. From the moment I arrived at the temple, Fulvia Pollo hated me. She accused me of breaking one rule after another and then finally she said she'd seen me with a man – something punishable by death. I swore it wasn't true but she wouldn't believe me and neither did any of the other vestals ... all except Marta. Marta was determined to help. Through you carrying messages, Marta and Rufus arranged my escape and just before I left, Marta told me what happened to your charm. I knew exactly where Fulvia Pollo kept her treasures so I stole it in case we ever met and I could repay you." Once more she held out her hand. "The charm is yours."

"Thank you." Gaius slipped it into the leather pouch hanging from his neck.

"Now that you know the whole story, let me apologize for what I forced you to do," said the tribune. "I hope you understand that I would have done things differently if there was any other way."

Gaius thought of Quintus. He would have done anything to help his brother ... He *did* understand.

"It's fine," he smiled. "I'm glad I could help."

"Good, and if ever you need help you must come to me."

Just then Zenobia returned with Zoe, looking sleepy and confused.

"With the slave and the charm our party is complete," announced General Marius happily. "We leave for Rome at dawn."

25

FOR weeks General Marius's army surrounded Rome's high stone walls, blocking the city's aqueducts and refusing to let anyone enter or leave. The city was running low on food and water, and in the hot summer sun the stench in its narrow lanes and alleys was unbearable.

"Soon the time will be right," General Marius said each day. "Soon even Sulla's most loyal followers will be desperate to escape."

One morning, after almost a month of the siege, Gaius woke early. He pulled himself off his trundle bed, doused his face with water and pulled on his tunic and sandals.

"Where are you going?" asked Alexander, propped up on the other bed and drowsily running a hand through his tangled black hair.

"For a walk. I love the camp at dawn."

"Wait and I'll come with you."

"And me," said Zoe. Since reaching the outskirts of Rome, Gaius had arranged for her to become his personal slave. The work was light and it meant that she slept just outside his tent rather than in the bleak slave dormitory. "I need to fetch fresh water."

They were soon strolling through a sea of white tents arranged in neat lines. After a while they reached a row of pens – pigs, cows and sheep to feed a hungry army.

"Let's head for the river," said Gaius.

They crossed a grassy field and clambered down a bank of reeds. Opposite, on the far side of the Tiber, a tunnel nestled below the city walls, its entrance almost hidden by ivy.

"I'll fetch the water here," said Zoe, wrinkling her nose. "That's the sewer and I don't want to be downstream of it."

She pulled up her brown tunic and waded into the murky river.

"Don't go too far," warned Gaius. "You'll be in range of soldiers patrolling the ramparts."

Zoe dipped her pail in the water and hurried back. "I wonder what it's like in the city," she said, staring at Rome's high walls.

"Awful," said Alexander, "and it will get worse. The place will go up in smoke when Marius attacks."

"You children are all looking very serious," said a deep voice behind them.

It was Rufus Agrippa, dressed in a crimson cape.

"You're up early, sir," said Gaius.

"Not early. I haven't been to bed yet. I've just finished my shift." He pointed to a small rowing boat moored a hundred yards downstream. "To make sure Sulla doesn't sneak out of Rome, the sewer is guarded at all times. It's my last shift tonight, thank the gods, as it's lonely work. Now do you want to get some breakfast? There's nothing like army porridge to start the day."

"Thank you, sir," said Gaius, "but we'll eat later."

"As you please. See you back at the camp." And then the tribune grinned mischievously. "Look who's coming! She can't seem to keep away from you."

Gaius's heart sank. Atia was weaving her way down the reed bank. Despite the early hour she was dressed in a floaty turquoise silk shift, her hair was elaborately braided and her lips stained bright red.

Not again, thought Gaius. When they'd reached Ostia, he had assumed that Atia would want no more to do with him, Alexander or Zoe but he was wrong. She seemed to pop up wherever they went, wanting to know what they were up to and whether she could join in.

"Why didn't you tell me you were going for a walk?" she whined.

"I thought you were still asleep."

"Not on an important day like this."

"What do you mean?"

Atia smiled, pleased to have aroused Gaius's interest. "Uncle has decided to attack Rome at dawn tomorrow. He wants you and Zoe at his side tonight when he asks for the gods' blessing. Just think! This time tomorrow we could be back in our own homes."

"If they're still there," murmured Alexander.

"Don't be such a misery. Anything has got to be better

than this camp." She turned to Gaius. "But I suppose you must be worried, with your mother being stuck in there."

"What?" said Gaius sharply.

"Didn't Marius tell you?" Atia put her hand theatrically to her lips. "Oops. I suppose he didn't want you to know in case you tried to rescue her. He heard yesterday that she is trapped in the city. She's been there for months and no one knows what shape she's in after all this time. You look upset. Have I said too much?"

"You said too much a while back," growled Alexander. "Clear off! All you do is cause mischief."

"How dare you speak to me like that!" said Atia.

"Go!" shouted Gaius furiously. "Now!"

"She could be lying," said Zoe as Atia stormed off. "You know what a troublemaker she is."

Gaius stared at the ramparts across the river. "No, she's right. I can feel it. And Marius is right too."

"What do you mean?"

"I will rescue Mother. It's time for Rufus Agrippa to return a favour."

26

"READY?"

Gaius, Alexander and Zoe were standing at the river's edge, ankle deep in cold water. It was close to midnight and the moon glowed dimly behind a veil of high cloud.

"Almost." Alexander threw a rope. "Zoe, climb in. Now you, Gaius."

As he clambered into the boat, Gaius was pleased to be on his way and very glad that Zoe and Alexander had insisted on coming too.

Alexander picked up the oars. "Are you both in?"

"Yes."

"Right, Zoe, push off."

Zoe stuck a long stick into the muddy riverbed and eased the boat forwards. A moment later it picked up a little of the current and then yanked to a halt.

"Has the rope caught?" asked Alexander, peering into the gloom. "Gaius, can you see anything?"

"No."

It was dark and still, the only sound the lapping of water against the hull of the boat, but then he made out the outline of a person at the water's edge, and they felt themselves being tugged the few feet back to shore.

"Oh no," said Zoe. "It's Atia."

"I knew you'd do something like this!" she said triumphantly. "Just wait until I tell Marius. You won't be the golden boy any more and that slave you're so fond of will be fed to the lions."

Gaius felt he would burst with fury. How dare this horrible girl stop him rescuing his mother?

"You're not going anywhere," he shouted, jumping out of the boat and wading ashore.

Atia turned and raced for the camp but Gaius was too quick for her. Before she'd reached the bulrushes he'd grabbed her wrist.

"You'll have to come with me," he said as he hauled her back to the boat. "And if you get killed, it will be your own fault."

Atia kicked and screamed. "How dare you? I'll have you beaten for this!" But he dumped her in the boat and pushed off once more.

"Marius will be furious! Let me go!"

"She's making so much noise she'll get us all killed if we don't shut her up," said Alexander, staring anxiously up at the ramparts.

Gaius knew Alexander was right.

"Atia, shut up!" he ordered but this only made things worse.

"No!" she shouted. "Turn this boat around or I'll scream until you do."

But Gaius knew he couldn't; he had to get into Rome.

Quickly he ripped a length of linen from his tunic and stuffed it in her mouth, and then grabbed a damp rope from the bottom of the boat.

"Zoe, help!"

Together they hurriedly tied knots around Atia's wrists and ankles. Atia's eyes bulged with fury but the only noise she could make was a low groan.

"That's better," said Gaius. "Row on."

Once more Alexander picked up the oars and rowed until the boat's stern crunched against the rocks of the far bank.

"Who's there?" called a gruff voice. It was Rufus Agrippa on patrol.

"It's Gaius. I need your help."

Quickly Gaius told Rufus Agrippa of his plan.

"Sulla's men are patrolling the city," said the tribune. "You could easily get caught. Your mother might be safer waiting rather than trying to escape with you."

"She won't be," said Gaius flatly. "I saw what happened when Sulla attacked last time."

The tribune sighed. "If you are really determined to do this I'll wait here and guard Atia. But remember, if you're not back by the time the first cockerel crows, you'll be caught in Marius's attack."

"I know," said Gaius. "We'll be as quick as we can."

Agrippa smiled ruefully. "The gods only know what General Marius will say when he finds out." He handed Gaius a torch and flint. "Light it once you're inside. Good luck."

The entrance to the tunnel was overgrown with ivy and was dank and dark. Gaius peered in and was immediately hit by the overpowering stench of sewage.

"Zoe, Alexander, are you sure you want to come too?" he gasped.

"Of course." Together they took one last deep gulp of fresh air and stepped into the foul tunnel.

"Here's the bathhouse door," said Gaius when they finally reached the entrance in the dripping stone wall. "No one will be around at this time of night. Come on."

The three children climbed the rock steps and found themselves in a long corridor. It was lined with shelves but instead of neat rows of bottles there was oil everywhere and the floor was covered in broken pottery.

"Remember how tidy it was before?" said Gaius. "Perhaps the bathhouse has been abandoned."

"It can't have been used for weeks," said Alexander. "Marius has switched of the aqueducts."

"There was plenty of water in the sewer," said Zoe.

"That's because it's an underground river. The baths use clean aqueduct water."

They hurried on, past a laundry room where towels were scattered across the floor, and reached a steep staircase. Suddenly Gaius stopped and held his finger to his lips. Footsteps were coming towards them from the floor above. Someone was in the building.

"We've got to hide," he whispered.

Quickly they retraced their steps, hearts pounding, but there was nowhere to take cover. Just in time they came to a laundry room and dived inside. At the back of the room, behind piles of strewn linen and grubby towels, were five large wicker baskets.

"Get in!" said Gaius, scrambling into one and pulling back the lid.

He crouched down on top of a bundle of dirty togas and sheets and tried to slow his heaving chest. He peered through a tiny gap in the wicker and saw two men standing in the doorway. One he recognized as Petronius, the fat bathhouse slave, the other was a slighter man also dressed in a slave's tunic.

"Petronius, it's late," whined the skinny man. "Let's come back in the morning."

"No. The rumour is that Marius will attack tomorrow. He could take the city by noon and if he does, I want the bathhouse to be ready for him. Pick up the dirty towels and put them in the baskets."

Within moments Gaius, Alexander and Zoe would be discovered – and there was nothing they could do about it.

27

GAIUS crouched down in his basket and pulled a clump of linen over his head as the slaves gathered up great piles of washing. He touched his charm and prayed, *Venus, help me.* Then the lid of his basket was lifted.

"Petronius, the baskets are full," complained the other slave. "No washing's been done for weeks."

The lid thumped back down.

"Try the others," ordered Petronius.

Gaius held his breath.

"They're all full."

Petronius sighed. "Let's clear up the corridor then. And I'll send for some slaves in the morning to sort this room out."

The door clicked shut. *We've done it,* thought Gaius jubilantly.

He climbed out of the basket and crept over to where Alexander and Zoe were hiding.

Zoe lifted her lid first. "How long will they be?"

"I don't know," said Gaius. "All we can do is wait."

They waited for what felt like hours. Every now and then Gaius opened the laundry room door a fraction but

Petronius and the other slave were always hard at work, sweeping and tidying.

At last he crept to the door and found the corridor empty.

"We can go," he whispered. "Let's hurry. We don't have much time."

As the three children ran through the deserted alleys of the Subura district the sky was turning grey. *Almost there*, Gaius said to himself. *We must get out of the city before Marius's attack begins.*

They reached the gates of his home and Gaius gently pushed open the unguarded door. The yard was just as he'd left it on the night of Sulla's attack – full of rubble and dust. For the first time it occurred to him that his mother might not be here after all, that she might have found somewhere else to shelter. And then in the far corner of the courtyard he noticed the faint glow of an oil lamp. There was someone in the kitchen.

"Wait here," he whispered to Alexander and Zoe.

He tiptoed across the atrium and peered through the kitchen window. Lying on a makeshift bed was a thin woman with greying hair. As she turned Gaius could see her high forehead and straight long nose and it dawned on him that this shrunken woman was his mother.

"Who is it?" said Aurelia nervously as he pushed open the door.

"It's me, Gaius!"

"Gaius?" She stared at him, ghostly pale. "Is it really

you? I've waited so long. I thought you'd been killed." She began to cry. "I've felt so awful all these months ... about the things I said to you when I heard about Quintus ... I didn't mean them ... I didn't know what I was saying. Can you forgive me?"

"Of course," said Gaius. "I forgave you as soon as you said them. But, Mother, Marius is about to attack. It's not safe. We must leave."

"How can we?"

"I know a way. But there's no time to lose."

He called Zoe to help his mother dress and in no time they were on their way. Aurelia took only one thing from her home – the tiny statue of Venus from the family altar. And the goddess must have brought them luck for they reached the entrance to the sewer without a hitch.

"The smell is awful," said Gaius, "but it's the only way out."

"Thank the gods," said Rufus Agrippa when they pushed the ivy aside and stumbled out of the tunnel below the ramparts. "The attack is about to begin. We must get across the river before it's too late."

They scrambled down the rocks and headed for the tiny rowing boat.

"Mother, get in," said Gaius. But as he held out his hand to help Aurelia, he felt a piercing pain in his head, as if someone were crushing his skull, and his mouth tasted horribly of iron.

His knees buckled and he collapsed to the ground.

28

GAIUS'S head was throbbing and every muscle ached.

"Can you hear me?" said a voice. It was Rufus Agrippa.

He was too exhausted to open his eyes but despite his grogginess he realized they must have got him across the river.

"It's just like last time," said his mother sadly. "I thought the gods had lifted this terrible curse but it's back."

"If the boy is cursed, nothing can be done," said Rufus Agrippa grimly.

"That's not true!" It was Alexander who was speaking and he sounded angry. "My father was a Greek doctor. He saw many cases like this and he could never understand the way you Romans treat them. Gaius doesn't have a curse; he has an illness. As long as care is taken each time he has a fit so that he doesn't hurt himself, he'll be fine. There's nothing to fear and nothing to be ashamed of."

"That may be what you Greeks believe," said Aurelia grimly, "but Gaius lives in Rome and we believe this curse comes from the gods."

"Then don't tell anyone, ma'am. I've known him for more than a year and I had no idea that he suffered from fits. If we're all sworn to secrecy, nobody will ever know."

"Your suggestion is impossible."

"So was rescuing General Marius last year, and now you, ma'am. Gaius couldn't have done these things if he were cursed by the gods. He could only do them with their blessing."

"What do you think, Aurelia?" Rufus Agrippa sounded doubtful.

Aurelia hesitated. "Gaius is descended from the goddess Venus and I've always been sure that one of my sons would return the family to glory, but look at him now..."

Gaius was terribly tired and he realized he must be very pale but he remembered something that Vestal Fulvia Pollo had said to him all those months ago in the temple... *Prove yourself worthy despite this affliction. Then you'll be remembered for something more.* Surely after all he'd been through in the past year he'd done that. There was more to him than this wretched curse. Using all his strength he opened his eyes and pulled himself up onto his elbows.

"Mother, it's over. I'm better now." He reached out and took her hand. "And there's something I must tell you."

"What is it?" she asked anxiously.

"After Vestal Fulvia Pollo sacrificed the lamb, she warned me that the curse would visit me again but she said that I shouldn't be frightened of it. Perhaps it is just an illness as Alexander says, or maybe it's something else, but either way I'm not scared any more and neither should you be."

Aurelia squeezed his hand and sighed. "Rufus Agrippa, I thought I'd lost both my sons. Now Gaius has been returned to me and I want to keep him by my side, but to do that I'll need your help. Will you keep our secret?"

"Of course," said the tribune. "If that's what you want."

"And you, Zoe and Alexander?"

"Yes."

"Then let us say no more about it. Atia is waking and it won't be long before the soldiers are here. General Marius once told me that he foresaw a great future for Gaius and my son deserves the chance to prove him right."

"I've no doubt he will," said Rufus Agrippa. "I've never met a braver boy."

29

AURELIA opened the gate to the courtyard.

"Take this to the kitchen," she said to Zoe, holding out a loaf of bread and a tired-looking leg of ham. "And Gaius and Alexander, don't do any more clearing up. The market will open soon and I can buy a couple of slaves to do it."

"Are you sure?" asked Gaius.

"Yes. The city is gradually returning to normal."

For two days, from the safety of the camp, Gaius had watched as Rome was bombarded with arrows, spears and catapults. General Marius's assault was merciless – it went on day and night and it wasn't long before a blanket of black smoke hung across the city.

At last, on the third day, to huge cheers from Marius's legions, the city gates swung open and Marius and his soldiers poured into Rome. Sulla was defeated and the war was over.

When at last they reached their home, Aurelia and Gaius discovered that they had been lucky. Part of the dining room had collapsed and a lump of concrete had smashed the courtyard floor, scattering brown and white mosaic tiles, but with work the villa would be habitable.

Gaius, Alexander and Zoe set to work straight away and

now, four days later, much of the Julii home was restored to normal. All they had left to do was clear up the mosaic tiles in the courtyard.

Zoe propped her broom up against a pillar and took the bread and ham into the kitchen.

"Please, Alexander, stop," said Aurelia, gently putting her hand on his arm. "You are our guest, not our slave. You have worked hard enough. Now rest and be assured you can stay with us as long as you wish. And as soon as things are more settled, we will help you search for your mother."

"Thank you," said Alexander gratefully.

"After all you have done for Gaius, it is nothing. Gaius, stop too. I have exciting news."

"What is it?" he asked, eagerly crossing the courtyard.

"The senators have begged General Marius to become Consul and he's agreed. It's his seventh term so you know what that means for us." She beamed. "The last egg has hatched and the Julii will rise again. Those vestals might be tricky, but they are never wrong. This evening we will go and thank them."

"Good." Gaius was delighted; he had a promise to keep. "And we must take Zoe."

"Why?"

"Trust me, Mother. You'll see it's the right thing to do."

An hour later Aurelia, Gaius, Alexander and Zoe entered the Forum. Although the wide, open square was still magnificent, the marble facades of the grand temples were pockmarked by missiles and many of their pillars were chipped.

Aurelia skirted the cracked steps of the Temple of Vesta and headed for the palace.

"If you want a light for your hearth, you must join the queue at the back of the temple," said a guard at the front door.

"We're here to see Vestal Fulvia Pollo," announced Aurelia. "Please tell her that Aurelia and Gaius of the Julii clan are here on urgent business."

"That's not possible, madam."

"Of course it is," snapped Aurelia. "If you're not careful, I'll report you to your centurion. Now do as I say, or I'll do it myself."

She was about to push open the heavy bronze door when out stepped a veiled woman.

"What's going on?"

"This woman is asking for Vestal Fulvia Pollo."

The vestal's head dropped. "Madam, you have not heard the sad news. Vestal Fulvia Pollo was killed in the battle for Rome. For now, I am in charge of the temple."

"I'm sorry," said Aurelia, blushing a little. "May I ask, madam, who you are?"

"Vestal Marta Publius."

Gaius's heart lifted.

"Vestal Marta, it's me ... Gaius Julius Caesar," he said hurriedly. "I've come to ask a favour."

"Gaius!" She stared at him through her white gauze veil. "You've grown so much, I didn't recognize you. Come inside, all of you. If you are friends of this boy you are welcome."

They entered a cavernous hall with grey marble walls, where Marta lifted her shroud to reveal a pale face and smiling blue eyes.

"What can I do for you, Gaius?"

"Not just for Gaius," interrupted Aurelia. "For the Julii family…"

"Let the boy speak," said Marta politely but firmly. "Gaius, what is it?"

Gaius turned and beckoned to Zoe, whose brown eyes widened in surprise.

"Someone once told me that you can free slaves. Is that true?"

"Yes, any vestal can, just by her touch."

"Then please free this one."

"Gaius, she's the only slave we have," said Aurelia, "and she's young and strong. We can't afford to let her go."

"I'm sure Gaius has his reasons," said Marta quietly.

Gaius took a deep breath and slowly, and in great detail, recounted the events of the past year. "So you see," he concluded, "Zoe saved my life many times. I promised to free her as soon as we got back to Rome. We arrived a few days ago and I don't want to leave it a moment longer."

"You are Zoe's owner, Aurelia," said Marta. "After all

that you've heard, do you still wish to keep her as your slave?"

"I suppose not," Aurelia mumbled.

"Good," said Marta. "Zoe, come here."

The slave stepped forward and Marta placed a hand on each of her shoulders. "By this touch you are free. Before you leave the temple this evening I will give you a letter that you must keep with you always. If any Roman challenges you, show it to them and they will let you go. If any Roman ever tries to enslave you again, show it to them and they will stop. Do you understand?"

"Yes," said Zoe, with tears in her eyes. "Thank you. And thank you, Gaius. I'm so happy."

"What will you do with this freedom of yours?" Marta enquired gently.

"The thing I've dreamt of since the day I was caught. I will go home to Thrace and tell my poor mother what happened to her children."

"Then I'm glad that I was able to help."

Marta made as if to usher them towards the door but Aurelia resisted.

"Madam, Zoe's freedom is not the only reason for our visit. We came to thank you and the gods. Vestal Fulvia Pollo told us that the Julii would only rise when General Marius became Consul once more. I had my doubts about whether this was possible but the Vestal Flame and the gods were wiser than me and we want you to know how grateful we are."

"It's not only the gods you have to thank," said Marta. "I understand that Gaius played his part."

"He did," said Aurelia, smiling with satisfaction. "He's a worthy son."

"He's more than that. He's a worthy Roman." Vestal Marta turned to Gaius. "You have succeeded despite great obstacles and you will do so again. You are a Roman that history will not forget."

"Thank you," said Gaius. And somehow he was certain it was true.

THE END

WHAT HAPPENED NEXT

IN 86 BC, after the defeat of Sulla, Marius was voted Consul of Rome for an historic seventh time, fulfilling the prophesy of his youth. A year later Gaius Julius Caesar joined the priesthood of Jupiter and married Cornelia Cinna, the daughter of Cinna, former Consul of Rome.

Meanwhile Sulla retreated to Greece, where he bided his time, waiting for revenge. In the summer of 83 BC, he marched on Rome once more. By this time Marius had died and after a bloody battle, Sulla overpowered the city and declared himself dictator. Voting in elections was abandoned, statues of Marius were destroyed and his body was exhumed and thrown into the River Tiber.

Each morning, in order to maintain control of Rome and terrify its citizens, Sulla posted a list in the Forum of those he wanted killed. Anyone with connections to Marius was especially vulnerable, but perhaps because of his position as a priest, Julius Caesar was not murdered. Instead he was given a choice: divorce Cornelia Cinna (daughter of an enemy of Sulla) or face death. Courageously, Julius Caesar refused to leave his wife. He disappeared into the countryside and a bounty was laid on his head. To avoid capture he moved from village to village but when his mother heard that he had contracted malaria, fearing he would be discovered, she turned to the Vestal Virgins for help. They begged Sulla to spare him and reluctantly the dictator agreed.

Although Julius Caesar was no longer hunted, he decided that it was wisest to stay away from Rome and so, at the age of nineteen, he joined the army. He served with distinction and bravery, earning the corona civica, an oak wreath crown awarded to the best soldiers.

Back in Rome, Sulla's cruel rule continued until he finally died of liver failure, probably caused by excessive alcohol.

With the death of Sulla, Julius Caesar was free to return to Rome. In 72 BC he was elected a military tribune and by 69 BC was a member of the Senate. Many military victories followed in Asia and Spain. During this period Cornelia Cinna died, probably in childbirth. Although he was often away fighting in the Roman provinces, Julius Caesar married twice more – first to Pompeia – whom he later divorced for adultery, and then to Calpurnia, the daughter of an aristocratic family.

While he was away, Rome was threatened from within. In one of the gladiatorial training camps a group of slaves seized knives from the kitchen, killed their guards and escaped. They were led by a charismatic man from Thrace – Spartacus.

There were thousands of slaves in Ancient Rome and when news of the uprising spread many decided to run away. Soon over a hundred thousand had joined

Spartacus's rebellion. The slaves fought their way north, hoping to escape Italy, and inflicted many defeats on the Roman army. At last they reached a port where Spartacus thought he could arrange their safe passage on ships, but pirates betrayed them, stealing their money and sailing off without a single one of them. The rebels were soon surrounded. During a final epic battle Spartacus was killed, and thousands of his followers were captured and later crucified. However, historians estimate that around five thousand slaves managed to escape and probably reached their homelands.

We do not know whether Julius Caesar played any part in defeating Spartacus's rebellion but we do know that by this time he was wealthy from the spoils of war. This allowed him to move his household from cramped rooms in the Subura district to a large mansion on the Sacra Via.

After a further period away in Spain, Julius Caesar returned home an honoured general and at the age of forty was elected Consul of Rome.

After his consulship he left for Gaul (modern-day France), and did not return home for nine years. This period established his reputation as one of the greatest generals of all time. Starting with only two legions he conquered all of Gaul, Helvetia (now Switzerland) and Germania (Belgium and parts of Germany), as well as leading the first invasion of Britain. As a result of his many victories he greatly increased the size of the Roman

Empire. During this period he also had several well-documented epileptic fits.

Julius Caesar's many triumphs on the battlefield, and the booty he sent back, made him a hero with Rome's citizens but not with their rulers. Powerful Romans were envious of his popularity. They decided to strip him of his powers by refusing to let him remain a soldier. After all Julius Caesar had done for Rome, this was a declaration of war. Forty years before, Sulla had started the First Roman Civil War by crossing the Rubicon River bearing arms. Julius Caesar now started the Second Civil War when he did the same on 10 January, 49 BC.

Julius Caesar easily defeated his aristocratic enemies and was subsequently elected Consul four times. While in office he pardoned his enemies, took land from rich landowners and gave it to poor soldiers, laid on lavish games and expanded the Roman Empire in North Africa, where he had a love affair with Cleopatra, the Egyptian queen. Effectively he became the first Emperor of the Roman Empire and was widely revered as a god, particularly as the Julii family were believed to have descended from the goddess Venus. All this aggravated the senators, who finally decided they must act.

On the morning of 15 March, 44 BC, Julius Caesar was, as usual, mobbed by petitioners as he made his way up the Senate steps. From out of the crowd stepped a senator called Cimber, who thrust a knife into his neck. Within moments other senators joined him, stabbing Julius Caesar with daggers hidden in the folds of their togas. The great warrior tried to escape but, blinded by blood, tripped on the stairs. There he was stabbed again and again as he lay defenceless. By the time his allies rescued him he was grievously wounded and died shortly after. He was fifty-six years old.

When the citizens of Rome heard what had happened to their hero they were outraged. They rioted, badly damaging the Forum and attacking the homes of any senator involved in the plot. The Third Roman Civil War had begun.

Despite having married three times, Julius Caesar had no legitimate children. In his will he surprised many by naming Octavian, a nineteen-year-old great-nephew, as his heir. It proved to be a wise choice. In the conflict that followed Julius Caesar's death, Octavian was a skilled politician and warrior, defeating his enemies and uniting Rome. Once peace was established, he declared himself Emperor, taking the title *Caesar Augustus* in honour of his great-uncle.

The empire Julius Caesar helped to create lasted over five hundred years. His legacy was so enduring that throughout history leaders have wanted to be associated with him. The French Emperor, Napoleon, had himself painted in the *corona civica* (the oak wreath crown) and studied Julius Caesar's battles in preparation for his own wars. Even in the twentieth century, two thousand years after his death, Russian kings were called *Czar* and German kings were known as *Kaiser*, both words derived from the name Caesar, and the many books, films and television programmes about his life ensure his legend lives on.

AUTHOR'S NOTES

WHEN I first began to research the early years of Gaius Julius Caesar's life I was surprised by how little scholars know. Early in the second century a Roman historian called Suetonius wrote a famous study of the lives of Rome's emperors and Julius Caesar was his first subject. However Suetonius wrote on fragile papyrus scrolls and the first scroll was lost or destroyed. Frustratingly, his study now begins, "In [Julius Caesar's] sixteenth year..." So although much is written about the adult Julius Caesar, very little is known about his childhood. It is not certain how many brothers and sisters he had and there is little evidence of how he survived Sulla's attack on Rome.

When writing this story I have tried to make sure that I have included the historical facts that are recorded and the key characters in Julius Caesar's early life. Sulla did invade Rome – the first Roman to cross the Rubicon bearing arms. Marius did become Consul for an historic seventh time and Spartacus was a slave who became a gladiator and later led a rebellion. Although these facts are agreed, I have, of course, had to imagine the characters of the main players. We do have some clues from the past. Marius often told the story of how, as a youth, he caught a nest with seven egret eggs in his garment and how he believed that this meant he was predestined to rule Rome seven times. Sulla was a vulgar man given to drinking and carousing. He also had a cruel, brutish streak. Spartacus must have been wilful and brave for he led a revolt knowing the punishment was crucifixion. And many sources confirm that Aurelia was convinced her children were descended from Venus and would one day rule Rome.

Lastly, Julius Caesar is described in a number of historical sources as being tall with fair skin, dark hair and piercing eyes. Contemporaries speak of his intelligence, liveliness, wit and charm. Perhaps because of his impoverished childhood he tried throughout his life to help the poor. He must also have been courageous. At the age of twenty he won the corona civica, only awarded for outstanding bravery, and went on to become one of the most successful soldiers the world has ever known.

Notes from the Past

THE BULLA: At nine days old, a Roman boy was named in a religious ceremony and then a charm, known as a bulla, was placed in a small leather bag and tied around his neck. This charm was supposed to ward off evil and was not removed until a boy reached fourteen. In wealthier families the charm was made of gold. In poor families it was made of silver or stone.

NAMES: Roman boys were given three names – a first name followed by the name of his clan and lastly the name of the family. Thus the name *Gaius Julius Caesar* would tell Romans that this boy was descended from the Caesar family, which itself was part of the Julii clan, and that his given name, and the name he would have been called by friends and family, was Gaius.

VESTAL VIRGINS: The Vestal Virgins were a Roman priesthood made up of six women. Their chief tasks were to maintain the fire sacred to Vesta, goddess of hearth and home, and to guard precious objects. They could also free prisoners and slaves just by touching them.

Vestal Virgins entered the priesthood at around the age of ten and served for thirty years. During this period they were forbidden from having any lovers. If a vestal broke this rule, she was buried alive.

SLAVERY: During Roman times slavery was accepted as a normal part of life. Romans captured slaves in conquered lands and shipped them back to Rome. Many slaves were children. They were often ill treated and worked long hours.

In aristocratic households there would be a large number of slaves. When they grew old some were freed by their wealthy masters as a reward for long service and many went on to settle in Rome.

CRUCIFIXION: This was a common punishment for slaves and criminals during the Roman era. A condemned man was flogged and then forced to pick up a heavy wooden cross and drag it to the outskirts of town. He was stripped and nailed to his cross by the roadside, usually suffering days of agony before dying of exhaustion.

In 73 BC, after the defeat of Spartacus, historians estimate that over six thousand slaves were crucified by the Romans as a punishment for their rebellion. Their bodies were displayed along the Appian Way, the main road through Italy.

Roughly one hundred years later Jesus was crucified. He lived in Judea (now modern-day Israel), then a Roman province. In AD 33, he was convicted in a Roman court of stirring up trouble in Jerusalem and was sentenced to this Roman punishment.

GLADIATORS: Fights to the death were a popular form of entertainment in Ancient Rome. Purpose-built arenas, such as the famous Colosseum, were constructed several years after Julius Caesar's death but before that, fights took place in the Forum, the busy square in the centre of the city. It would be filled with benches and its paving stones covered with sand to absorb the blood.

The main source of gladiators was slaves, particularly those deemed difficult or prone to running away. To enliven the show, they were given different sorts of armour and weapons – either nets or swords. Fights began with the Latin words, "Morituri te salutamus" or "We who are about to die salute you." A gladiator could beg for mercy by raising his index finger. It was for the host to decide his fate, however, spectators made their wishes known. A circle of the thumb and first finger meant mercy whereas a thumb pointing down meant death. These signs are still used to mean "good" and "bad".

HEALTH: Romans had little understanding of how the body worked. Life expectancy was short and disease was common due to poor diet, lack of medical care and hard living conditions.

Traditionally Roman doctors relied on charms and offerings to the gods. The more expensive the gift, the more it was prized. Examples include gladiator's blood, human fat and the brains of babies.

Around 200 BC the Romans realized that Greek doctors were more advanced in their understanding of the health benefits of some herbs and salts and their cures became fashionable. In 46 BC Julius Caesar granted Roman citizenship to all Greek doctors in recognition of their skills.

EPILEPSY: Julius Caesar suffered from epilepsy. This illness is caused by unusual activity in the brain that results in a person having seizures, sometimes known as epileptic fits. During a seizure the body becomes stiff, the arms and legs twitch and the person falls unconscious. A seizure usually lasts between one and three minutes.

People who have epilepsy often sense when a fit is on its way. These warning signs, known as auras, include a strange taste in the mouth, a feeling that the world has become dreamlike and strange sensations in the limbs.

CAESAREAN: It is often said that Julius Caesar was born by Caesarean section. This is unlikely to be true. During Roman times, cutting a child from a mother's womb was only undertaken in extreme circumstances such as when a mother had died in labour. This is because the procedure resulted in almost certain death for the mother. Aurelia lived for fifty years after Julius Caesar's birth and so is unlikely to have gone through this ordeal.

PLUMBING AND SEWERS: The Romans were great builders and engineers. They were the first people to construct aqueducts, which carried water many kilometres from the mountains to their cities and provided water for public fountains, bathhouses and public toilets through an elaborate system of lead pipes. The Romans also built a series of sewers to keep their cities clean. They were such good engineers that the sewer under Rome can still be walked through today.

In around AD 500, when the Roman Empire ended, their plumbing and sewerage systems fell into disrepair. Once again European towns had no running water and were beset by human waste and dirt. It was not until the Victorian era, thirteen hundred years after the fall of Rome, that Europeans once again enjoyed the benefits of clean, fresh water and a sewage system to take waste away.

CALENDAR: The names of our months have Roman origins. Early Romans divided the year into ten months – *Martius*, *Aprilis* and *Maius* (all named after Roman gods and now known as March, April and May), followed by *Quintillis*, *Sextillis*, *September*, *October*, *November* and *December* (meaning the fifth month, the sixth month etc., up to the tenth month, December). Later two extra months were added at the start of the year – *Januarius* and *Februaris*.

After Julius Caesar's assassination, *Quintillis* was changed to *Julius*, our modern July, in his honour. Later still *Sextillis* was changed to *August*, in memory of Augustus, the first official Roman Emperor and Gaius's great-nephew.

DAYS OF THE WEEK: A number of our days also have Roman origins. Romans divided the week into seven days, named after the sun, moon and the planets. Three of these names survive in modern English – *Saturni* (after Saturn and now Saturday), *Solis* (meaning sun, now Sunday) and *Lunal* (meaning moon, now Monday). The other four days were *Martis* after Mars, *Mercuri* after Mercury, *Jovis* after Jupiter and *Veneris* after Venus. Although modern-day versions of these survive in French, Italian and Spanish, the English names – Tuesday, Wednesday, Thursday and Friday – honour Norse gods and were adopted during Viking times.

Before they were famous ... meet Cleopatra, who will one day be the Queen of Egypt.

As a young girl she flees Alexandria, fearing for her life. Living in hiding, uncertain of her future, she finally receives news from home. The time has come to face her enemies – and take her place as Princess Cleopatra, future Queen of Egypt.

BY CAROLINE CORBY

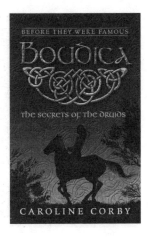

Before they were famous ... Meet Boudica, one day to be England's warrior queen.

As a tribesman's daughter in Ancient Britain, Boudica is in trouble. The Romans have invaded, her father has been accused of murder and she doesn't know who to trust. When a mysterious druid appears in her village, she knows she must enter his murky world if she is to bring honour to her tribe.

By Caroline Corby

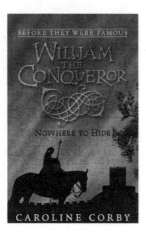

Before they were famous ... Meet Willam, one day to be William the Conqueror, Duke of Normandy.

Medieval France is shocked when the son of a peasant is chosen as Duke of Normandy. Powerful families plan to murder the boy and steal his title. He runs for his life, but when there's nowhere else to hide, it's time to face his enemies and become William the Conqueror.

BY CAROLINE CORBY

Before they were famous ... Meet Pocahontas, who saved the first English colony in Virginia and shaped the destiny of her people for ever.

The Native Americans of Virginia had a prophecy – that one day strangers would come to Chesapeake Bay and destroy them. So when a group of English settlers land, Chief Powhatan forbids his people to approach them. But his daughter Pocahontas is too curious to obey. Are the mysterious pale men to be trusted or will the terrifying prophecy come true?

By Caroline Corby

Before they were famous... Meet Jane, who will one day be Queen of England.

When King Henry VIII dies, young, aristocratic Lady Jane Grey finds herself heir to the throne. Abandoned by her family, she falls into the hands of a wicked duke and her fate is sealed. Lady Jane Grey must become queen or die.

BY CAROLINE CORBY